Forever Friends;

The Good, The Bad,
The Beach.

By

L. Martell

Dedication

To My best friend, Misty,

Thank you for every adventure you have ever dragged me into. Without you, I would have never found my true self. Soulmates do come in friend form. And that is what we are. Forever Friends, Sisters always ♥ I love you.

Acknowledgement

To my Husband & son for putting up with my sleepless nights writing & working. Thank you for supporting my dreams always. You guys are my world. None of this would be possible without your support. ♥

To my aunt Jackie. You have always been my best friend. Thank you for supporting every dream I've ever had since I was a little girl. I couldn't have done it without you.

About the Author

L. Martell is a wife & mother from New England. L cares for her senior puggle & works full time .

She finds joy in reading & writing. Her favorite genres include Romance, Historical Fiction, Fantasy, & more. L's hope is to share her writing & let others enjoy a nice break from reality.

Table of Contents

Chapter 1

I met my husband when I was 15 years old. Most people call it love at first sight, but little do they know it was disgust at first sight. Not only was wearing an old Van Halen T Shirt with his long shaggy hair, but he was smoking a cigarette. Gross. I was what some may call a "prissy" girl. I was always well kept, well dressed, & well mannered. I hardly ever swore, I was always home by 9pm, & I certainly never smoked a cigarette. We were total opposites. But you know what they say about opposites, they attract, marry, produce off spring, & divorce.

The sound of the loud bus horn snapped me out of my day dream. I turned the sink off & looked down at the water flowing over the coffee carafe.

"Clara, Carson… let's go, the bus is not going to wait forever." This was the first year Carson would go to away camp with his sister. My youngest baby is officially old enough for away camp with his big sister. Carson turned 10 in May. Just making the cut off for Summer Slumber Camp in Hollinsworth. Four full weeks without my kids in the house. My first summer alone since the divorce. Sure our divorce was technically finalized a year ago but I have not spent this long alone since… "Mom have you seen my headphones?" Clara says.

I look over my shoulder "table" I say.

Clara grabs her headphones, slings her baby pink duffle bag over her shoulder & hugs me tight. "Mom don't cry, I have gone to camp before you know." she says. I smile & kiss her forehead. Keep an eye on your brother for me & stay close to the camp leaders. I love you Clara Paige. "I know, I know, love you too mom." Clara runs down the front steps without looking back. Clara is 12 so she has been going to camp for 2 years now. She loves Summer Slumber Camp.

"Hi mom, bye mom" Carson bolts out from the bathroom with his star wars back pack, his green stuffed bear & his yellow kick ball. "Excuse me Carson Russell Paisley." I say. Carson stops, drops his stuff & runs into my body with open arms. "Sorry mommy, I love you, I am so excited to go to slumber summer camp." I smile & hold him closely. "I know you are. Please be good & listen to your group counselor & all the camp leaders. Stay with a buddy at all times & check in with your sister when you can." I kiss him on the cheek & forehead & he smiles & turns on his heels.

Carson grabs his snack bag I packed for him & Clara's since she took off without it & runs out. I wave goodbye from the porch as the bus pulls off.

I walk into a silent kitchen & an empty house. I pour myself a cup of coffee as I notice it has brewed while I was seeing the kids off. I sit down with the intent to write out some bills & look at the schedule for the week ahead. Tomorrow is July 8th I noticed on the calendar. My wedding anniversary.

~~~~~~

"Hey, you ever smile?" I look up from my book & see his long hair & his scruffy face looking at me. "Excuse me" I say. He laughs & shakes his head. "I said, you ever smile?" How rude. Who says something like that to a total stranger. I smile, little does he know I happen to have won best smile in our 8th grade class nominations. I roll my eyes at the question but answer. "Yes, of course I do" I say in an abrupt tone. He flicks his smoke on the ground & smiles at me. "I see you walking by everyday, you always look so serious. So I was wondering if you ever flash a smile." His cocky attitude was not
~~~~~~

~~~~~~~~~~~~~~~~~~~~~~~~~~~~~~~~~~~~

The phone ringing brings me back to reality. I look at my cell phone. "Mya" lights up on the screen. My best friend. I hit answer & groan into the phone "Hey Mya". I hear a screech on the other end.

"LANA, summer is here, time for a loud mother effing cheer. Did the kiddos get picked up yet or what?" she says. "Yes Mya, my Clara & Carson have left for slumber camp an hour ago." I reply. She sighs "My goodness a whole hour ago, why are we not 3 mimosas deep then at Bradly's Brunch & Brew?" she asks. "Well Mya, for starters its 11am, and as I have said before I am not day drinking with you we are 32 years old." Mya's tone changes. "Lana, I am 31 remember?"

Mya is 6 months younger than me & she never lets me forget it. Mya has been my best friend for as long as I can remember. Childhood friends. My only friend. Aside from Amy, but I suppose sisters don't count. They are born to like you & be your friend. I shake my head & smile because that's all you can do when you are talking to Mya. Smile. "What are you up to Mya? Shouldn't you be working by now?" I ask. "I took off the entire week & guess what we are going to do. We are going to spend your free time getting your groove back! I have a plan." She says.
~~~~~~~~~~~~~~~~~~~~~~~~~~~~~~~~~~~~

As someone who has known Mya almost 20 years. I can tell you right now it is never a good idea when Mya has an idea. "Mya, my love. I have plans this week. They do not involve drinking, guys, or dancing." I say.

Mya laughs but then gets serious. "Let me guess Lana, they involve books, sweats, & blueberry scones. Lana you are 32 not 62. You need to get back out there. Derek left 2 years ago. It is time you get back out there & meet someone." She says.

Usually, Mya is very blunt but this morning she is irritating me a little more than usual. I am assuming she doesn't realize tomorrow would be my 13-year wedding anniversary.

"Mya, I think I know what is best for me." I say as I roll my eyes.

"Well as your best friend Lana Edith Harper Paisley - please drop Derek's stupid last name, I know what's BETTER for you. So pack your bags because we are heading to Kirkland Beach for the next 5 days! I will be there by 2pm to pick you up." She screams.

I dropped my scone on my plate. "Kirkland......Beach" I say. I sigh & put my head in my hand. I cannot believe she is dragging me to Kirkland Beach. Of all places. Kirkland Beach. She is done for when I see her.

Chapter 2

I hate what I see when I look in the mirror. I look so old. I have gained a good 20 lbs. since the divorce. I sigh & look in my closet. I have no idea what to even pack because I am pretty sure pink floral pajama bottoms & black leggings are not proper beach attire. I stop & stare at the back rack in my closet. My yellow bikini hangs on a rack. Derek bought me that as a joke because we used to love the "itsy beets teeny weeny yellow polka dot bikini" commercial. Next to that is my white one-piece mom style bathing suit dress. I grab the white bathing suit & pack it in my bag. I look around for a few sun dresses & some shorts & sneakers. I sigh again with my hands on my hips I look around. "5 days away with my best friend, I suppose this has potential. The idea is promising. If my sweet, loveable best friend behaves herself. Unlikely."

I grab my phone to see if Clara or Carson has text me. It is about 12 noon. They should just be arriving at camp & unloading the bus. Bing Bing Bing – a text comes across the screen from Mya. "Hitting the corner café, what do you want?" When Mya says the corner café, she also means the corner store. She will surely be getting drinks for both day & night. One thing about Mya, she knew how to have a good time & she especially knew how to pick you up when you were down. I will never forget the night Derek told me the truth. If it wasn't for Mya, I most likely would not have survived that night.

I text back "Ice coffee, almond milk" I reply. I look in the mirror one more time & sigh. I text again "Oh, and one of those banana biscotti." I put my phone down & go back to the mirror. My dark curly hair is looking awfully gray. Well there are 8 gray hairs to be specific. I pluck them out daily. They come right back. I swear it is my Nonna Razza haunting me because I married Derek. I stare harder at myself in the mirror. My once curvy, beautiful body is looking very jiggly. My once pearly white teeth are looking like years of coffee stains. I sigh and walk away from the mirror disappointed in what I see. I look down at my suitcase & begin my checklist. 4 mom approved swimsuits, all one-pieces with cover ups, check. Yoga shorts with pockets & matching tops. Check. 2 black dresses, check. 1 yellow sundress for fun check. And of course, my pink floral pajamas. Old faithful. Check. Now onto my toiletries bag.

<p style="text-align:center">~~~~~~~~~~~~~~~~~~~~~~~~~~~~~~~~~~</p>

"Lana, wait up". I hear a voice calling from the crowded hallway. It is him. Will he never get the hint. How many times do I have to avoid this guy. I roll my shoulders & try to shimmy through the crowd unnoticed. "Lana, Lana, LANA" I look to my left & see Mya screaming my name. Even if I wanted to fly under the radar it would be impossible now since my loud mouthed gorgeous best friend just let all of New England know where I was. "Jeesh, how many times do I need to call before you come to me my little book worm." My says sarcastically. I drop my book to my side & shake my head at her. I look up and see him getting closer and closer. I grab Mya's arm and drag her off to the side. "Did you not see I was trying to be stealth." I whisper. She laughs and looks over my shoulder at the tall rocker guy waving me down. "I sure hope it was not because you are afraid of sir rocks a lot." She laughs so hard she almost screams. I turn around and see him standing right behind me. "Damn, you hard of hearing or are you just ignoring me in plain sight." I roll my eyes & look at Mya then him. "I was kind of talking to my best friend, so I wasn't really doing anything." I say standoffishly. He looks me up & down my navy sweater is wrapped around my shoulders and he smiles. "It is okay to come to school without that sweater around your shoulders you know. It is the middle of April. I think the cold weather is passed." He laughs & shakes his head. My face turns red & the steam is coming from my ears. Before I can say anything Mya

6

interjects. "Look rock em sock em robot, we are kind of in the middle of a conversation here. It involves A & B so kindly C your way out." She says as she grabs my arm & begins to walk away. He grins & watches us walk away, I turn back to see he is still standing there when he yells "I will see you tomorrow morning Lana, same time, same place." I turn my head & keep walking with Mya.

The door swings open & in walks Mya.

"Well, well, well look who decided to dress up. Honestly Lana isn't that Grandma Harpers sweater. It is friggin July. Cut the shit before I make you wear my mesh dress."

I roll my eyes, "come on in Mya, is that the key you made yourself to my house."

She looks at me while she opens my fridge, "as a matter of fact this is the one Clara gave me since I lost the other one." She says with a grin.

I look up at her with shock on my face. "You lost my HOUSE KEY MYA?" She turns back to the fridge & ignores me. "What can we mix vodka, tequila, rum, whiskey, & gin with?" She laughs & closes the fridge. When she turns around luckily I notice she only has a bottle of water in her hands. "Very funny Mya. Do not think for one second that just because I agreed to go with you means I am going to be getting wasted like a high school girl on her spring break with you." She rolls her eyes & dumps her water down my sink. She pulls a small bottle of strawberry flavored vodka from her purse & begins to pour it into the bottle.

"A. you did not agree to anything, I gave you no say in the matter. B. I am fully planning on you getting wasted because, well, you cannot hold your alcohol so a sip of these & you will be the life of my party. And C. shut up, do what I say & please take off your grandmothers friggin sweater Lana. God." She says.

I smile at her & laugh. "I miss them you know. Grams & Nonna."

Both of my grandmothers passed away about 3 years ago. First was Nonna Razza & then Grandma Harper. Grandma was my best friend in the entire world. I didn't really get along with my parents but my grandmothers were the next best thing to parents. I lived with both of my grandmas. They had become best friends when my parents married. Even long after they divorced. They bought a house together near my parents when Nonno passed. Gramps had unfortunately passed before I was even born so I never met the rascal that stole Grams heart. But my Nonno was the love of Nonna's life. My mothers parents were straight from Italy. Married since 16 and madly in love. A beautiful thing. True love. Everyone's dream.

Mya never looks up but I can feel her energy. "I know you do, I do too." Mya lived with me & my grams for a bit after her parents passed away. She was 16 but I know she still feels the pain deeply. Though she will never show it because another thing about Mya, she is a closed book I like to call her. Mya will never let her emotions out because she does not want to be seen as weak. Although nobody could ever call her weak. Mya has accomplished more then anyone I have ever known & she did it all alone. I may have given her a few words of wisdom along the way, but that girl is fearless, courageous, & vivacious. I aspire to be like her in many aspects of my life. I drop my head & shake off the glum feelings. "So, 5 days in Kirkland Beach, and why did you think this was a good idea for ME of all people to go to Kirkland Beach Ms. Mya Penelope Rogers?" I ask. Mya looks up at me with a scary smile, I have seen that smile before. "Because, you Lana Edith Harper – name I will not say anymore, are going to get your groove back!"

Chapter 3

I look down at my phone to see Carson sent me a sunglasses emoji with a heart. I send him a text back "I love you too my cool camper. With a smiley emoji." I drop my phone & look over at Mya, why did I agree to this trip. How did I end up driving, & where the heck is this girls luggage? "Mya", I say. "Where is your luggage?" I asked her. She starts to laugh hysterically & I am afraid to ask her what is so funny. I turn the radio down & look at her. She motions to my back seat. I see a black & pink plaid bag on the floor in the back. "Mya, do you have a key to my car too!?" she laughs & turns up the radio.

It takes us 45 minutes to get to Kirkland Beach from our town. It was almost an hour with traffic but we arrive at Kirk's Castle resort. The top resort on the beach. 5 nights here must have cost Mya an arm & a leg. We might as well buy a small home for this price. I look up to see 3 men in Hawaiian shirts coming over to my car. "Welcome to Kirk's Castle Resorts, Bill will valet park, and Jonah & I will escort you ladies in. "Luggage?" he asks. Mya opens the back door & grabs her two bags & swings them over her shoulder. Mya will not let a man carry her bags for her. She is too independent for that, buy her a drink a little later maybe. But not carry her bags. I look over my shoulder at my 2 suitcases. One has wheels, one is carry case bag. "I think we can manage alright." I say.

"No problema senorita, right this way." The tall guy says to us. We follow behind the men & walk into the lobby. It is stunning. Tall ceilings, gorgeous glass windowpanes down to the floor. Beautiful gold décor & a big water fountain right in the center of the room. I look over at Mya who has somehow found her way to the lounge. She smiles & winks at mc & walks back to over my way. "Okay, she says got that out of the way, reservation for 9pm for us," she says. I look her straight in the face & laugh. "9pm ….. Mya, for dinner? It is 4pm right now. Why not get settled in the room & then grab a dinner & explore the amenities," I say.

She rolls her eyes & walks right by me. "Checking in for Rogers" she says. "Mya Rogers, double queen suite, beach view" the woman reads back to her. "That's us," she smiles.

Chapter 4

I plop down on the queen size mattress all for myself. I look around at the gorgeous ocean view & my beautiful best friend who is smiling in the mirror holding dress after dress up to herself. "Shouldn't you be wearing bikini's and flip flops at the beach Mya, you look like you're getting ready for a 5 star restaurant & dance party." I say smiling.

"Well, I want to see what dress I am wearing to the lounge tonight. Duh, that's what's most important here. Not the beach. We need to meet a guy for you." Mya looks at me devilishly. "You need this, I need this, WE NEED THIS. Tell me the truth, how long has it been since you've had some real, raunchy action?" Mya asks.

I look over at her & burst out laughing. "Mya, seriously how old are you raunchy action? HA. Have I ever had any raunchy action? And anyways, that's neither here nor there. I decided to come to relax & enjoy the beach, the hotel, the amenities, the quiet." I say.

She turns back around to look at herself in the mirror & sighs. "Well if you wanted quiet, you should have booked your own room. This isn't Miami, and we are not a couple of old ladies who are going to share a cheesecake at midnight tonight. Because come midnight tonight the only thing I might be sharing is my body with the hot valet guy downstairs." Says Mya.

I look over to her my cheeks flushed, "MYA PENELOPE, please I beg of you…. Go back to his room. Don't do this to me again." She winks at me & throws a short red dress at me. "Put this on, it will fit you perfectly. And please do something with your hair other than a high bun, I say this because I love you & you have better hair then me." She says sweetly.

I look down at the very short, very low cut, very sheer red dress on the bed. I sigh & stand to look in the mirror once Mya has gone to bathroom to start her 2 hour long journey of getting ready. I see the bags under my eyes. I see the love handles hanging over my jean shorts. I see my worry lines and my crows' feet. I put my head down & walk away when my phone goes off. I look up & run to check the message in case its from one of the kids. "Exxxxxxxx" lights up. Yes, I realize it's very dramatic & immature to have him saved under that name but he annoys me.

"Hey sunshine, check your Parent's of Slumber page – the camp counselor just tagged you in an awesome picture of Clara and Carson setting up the welcome flags."

Reads the text from Derek. I smile thinking of my babies enjoying themselves.

I look out the window at the gorgeous sky as the sun is just starting to go down & I think about my babies. How lucky I was to have two kids who got along so well. No fights, and they always looked after each other & played together. They were angels, & I was blessed. I always wanted a big family. I would have had more kids if Derek would've. He told me one boy & one girl was perfect. And since we had the kids so young, he said we should slow down & maybe try for a third later on. Obviously later never came. I looked at my phone again & reply to Derek. "Will do Captain, I am away for a few days with Mya. Thanks for the update." Derek always called me Sunshine, & I called him Captain. Inside jokes we had. He is also the only person who calls me L & I call him D. I guess some things never changed for us. Others certainly did. Like his address & his relationship status. Derek has been in a serious relationship with Maritsa for about 8 months now. They recently moved in together & he introduced her to Clara & Carson. Maritsa is a 27-year-old salsa instructor at the local community center. She is also an online model & a vegan. She must be by far the most beautiful woman I have ever seen. She is tall & skinny with a great ass. Not that I was looking but it's hard to miss. A lot nicer than mine. I guess when you have kids the old body never comes back. No wonder he left me for her. It makes sense, it just doesn't seem real. I look down at my phone to see one last message from Derek. **"Away with Mya, jeez L, behave."** I roll my eyes and put my phone down. It's no secret that Derek & Mya dislike each other. Especially since the divorce was finalized. I do not think there is a person Mya dislikes more in this world. Aside from her own ex loser of a boyfriend.

"Hello, earth to Lana, are you ready or are you stalling?" she says. Out comes Mya in this adorable cheetah print romper. If I was a guy, I would migrate towards her in a crowded room. Oh yeah. She looks incredible. And she wants me to go out & stand next to her. I am mortified. My body is nothing compared to hers. She is a goddess in many ways. I wish I had her confidence. She walks into a room & shines. I walk into a room & have an anxiety attack. I smile at her "Wow My, you look ferocious as usual." Mya looks at me & laughs. "Get the red dress on Lana we are going prowling." She says.

<h1 style="text-align:center">Chapter 5</h1>

I look in the mirror in the bathroom & try to pin my gray hairs down so nobody can see them. Sure there are only a few but I want them hidden. My dark bangs hide my bushy eyebrows thank gosh. I paint my lips with the nude pink lip stain from my make up bag & I brush my eyelashes with the triple volume mascara I have & tug the red dress down one more time before I turn to head out.

Mya stands at the bathroom door about to knock when I open the door. "Mhm, I knew you'd look good in that dress, it was made for you." Mya says devilishly. I am blushing & I look down at my bare feet. "I suppose my white crocs are a no go with this dress." I say.

Mya winks at me & says "5 steps ahead of you, as always." She hands me a pair of black stiletto heels with a little bow on the side. I look at her, laugh & say "Well, I sure hope you will be the one wearing those shoes. I don't feel like falling & breaking anything tonight." She gives me the side eye. "Lana, put the shoes on & let's go." I sigh, but do it. I take one step & try to adjust my legs to the added height from the heels. I fix myself one last time, grab my purse & Mya leads us out the door.

The hotel lobby is more crowded than when we arrived. There are so many people down here for the night life. The hotel lobby is even more beautiful in the evening than in the daylight. There are twinkling lights shining all along the glass floor length windows. There are gorgeous chandeliers with pure gold candelabras & bright lights beaming from the ceiling. The lounge, however, is dark & exclusive. The line to get inside is not to long & the man at the door is checking the names off the list for reservations. I can hear soft music coming from there. It seems to be elegant. Luckily not what I was thinking it might be, especially knowing Mya can be adventurous in the types of clubs she tries. This seems like it might be alright after all. May even be actual fun.

We get up to the entrance to the lounge & Mya gives the guy at the door our names. "Mya Rogers, party of 2 9pm." She says. He nods to us & unclips the velvet rope blocking our way inside. Mya pushes through the red curtains blocking our view & I am mesmerized by what I see. This is nothing I thought it would be. There are people everywhere dancing, drinking, talking. I had no idea this lounge even extended this far back. There are very dim lights all along the wall. Beautiful sconces, about 15 of them on each side lining down the walls. They are elegant & gorgeous. The tables are covered in deep red tablecloths that look more expensive than anything I ever owned. And that's just the tablecloths. The bar is a gorgeous black & gold marble that shimmers in the dim lighting. The gold flecks are so pretty it looks like real gold.

I am drawn suddenly to the big black piano at the end of the bar. It is stunning & huge. I do not play piano, but I love to listen to live piano. Derek & I once went to this restaurant & they played piano while we ate. It was so soothing & enjoyable. I loved it. The sound of a piano is comforting to me.

I look to the dance floor & the ages look mixed. Some people may be my age, some younger & a few older. The majority seems to be 21-35. If I had to guess, then again it is dark in here. "Let's grab some drinks & start to mingle. Who is buying the first round? NOT IT." Mya says loudly over the growing noise the deeper we go into the lounge.

I smile & hold up my clutch & wave it in front of her face. "I got it don't worry." I say.

I wink & say "let me guess something with tequila, vodka, rum & anything else they've got back there." Mya winks back & says "precisely."

I walk over to the bar & see two bartenders. Both young men. I wave one of them over & order two vodka sodas with lime. I look around & spot Mya already dancing on the floor to some new Beyonce song. She is such a light. I wish I could be more like her. Lately I feel like a storm cloud of darkness. I guess it is expected after everything I have been through.

"So, let me get this straight you won't be my girlfriend, but you will go out with me?" Derek shakes his head in confusion & stares me down. "I am not allowed to have a boyfriend right now Derek. But we can hang out sometimes. Why isn't that good enough?" I say. Derek smiles at me sweetly. "I want you to be my girlfriend, I am crazy about you Lana. I am falling for you." He says. I look around checking to see if anyone is listening. My cheeks are rosy pink, almost red. I smile softly & look at him. "I really like you too Derek. But I cannot disobey Nonna Razza's rules. She told me no dating until senior year." Derek grabs me & looks into my eyes & says, "So don't tell Nonna Rozza, just tell me. Tell me you will be my girlfriend. Tell me that you ARE my girlfriend." I smile at Derek and plant a small kiss on his cheek. "I am yours Derek. I am yours."

I snap back to reality when the bartender asks if I want to open a tab or pay cash. I give him my credit card & tell him to open a tab & hold my card. Mya paid for 5 nights at this place which I imagine is damn expensive. The least I can do is buy dinner & drinks all week. I grab our drinks & walk over to Mya. She is standing in the middle of the floor wiggling her finger & calling me towards her. I slowly walk towards her & hand her a drink. I can barely make out what she is saying over the music but she has the biggest smile on her face. It is hard to be all doom & gloom with Mya around. She makes it hard to not have a good time. I smile at her & take a sip of my drink & begin to dance with her. I am not sure what song is playing but the rhythm sounds marvelous. A few moments go by & two guys walk over to us. I am not surprised considering what we are wearing.

Mya pulls me close & whispers in my ear, dibs on tall dark & handsome in the white. I look at them & they are both tall dark & handsome. However, the one in the blue button down is a lot more handsome I notice as he gets closer to us.

"Hey, you ladies like a drink?" The one in the white t shirt says.

"Sure, but only if you are buying." Says Mya. Again, her confidence is very admirable. I stay silent while I let her do all the talking. But I listen attentively to make sure the conversation stays somewhat appropriate.

Sometimes Mya tells me I act like her mom. But I do not mean to. Truth is growing up I always felt like she was another sister to me. Sure, I had Amy but growing up Amy & I had a big age gap. When Mya & I were in high school Amy was just finishing elementary school. So, while Mya & I drooled over boy bands & the hottest make up trends, Amy wanted to play playground games & go see PG rated movies. And Mya lost her parents at only 16. Not like they were ever around for her the way parents should be. Always jetting off on their own adventure. I see where Mya gets it. But Mya was their only child & they left her with her grandmother at a young age. But Mya migrated to Nonna's house where I was & she basically lived with us & grew up with us. Mya was at every holiday & was just as much part of the family as any of us. Both Nonna Razza & Grandma Harper treated her no differently.

As the years went on & Grams & Nonna passed away it was just us girls. Me, Mya, & Amy who is currently doing what she should be doing at college. She is taking summer courses & working on campus to pay for her school.

"Lana, hello…… vodka soda? Or want to take a shot with me & Fabio?" Mya says & snaps me out of my train of thought. The guy in the t shirt looks over at her & laughs. "My name is JC." he says loudly over the music & background noise. Mya looks over her shoulder & smiles, "I know, but I will probably call you Fabio all night. So let's just accept that & move on now."

There goes that incredibly confident attitude of hers. I smile & say "I am still drinking my current drink. Maybe in a few." I say. Mya turns her head & looks at the two guys, then back at me. "FOUR SHOTS OF TEQUILA, COMING UP!" she says to JC.

I just shake my head & look at the guy in the blue button down. He stares at me & takes a sip of his beer. "Not a big drinker I take it." He says to me.

I look over at the bar at Mya & JC ordering 4 shots of what I assume is tequila like she said. But then again. This IS Mya we are talking about.

"I am not really much of a going out type of person in general." I say.

With instant regret as I see his eyebrow raise & he takes another sip of his drink. He looks at me for a minute, up & down checking out my attire & body I assume. Great. I am sure by now the red dress is so far up he can see the jiggly parts of my thighs. I blush a bit & go to ask his name, but he interjects. "I am not big on the club scene either. I prefer a more intimate or quiet setting. I only drink beer occasionally to be social. Especially with this guy." He says & nods his head toward the bar at JC. I laugh because it sounds just like me & Mya.

"My name is Lana. It's nice to meet you." I say & put out my hand to shake his. He smiles & grabs my hand gently. "It's nice to meet you Lana, you have quite the etiquette. My name's Henry." I smile so hard I feel like I am getting an injection of Botox. I am not sure if it's because I feel very awkward or if because my vodka soda is officially gone & I may be feeling slightly buzzed. Before I can say anything else Mya & JC come back & thrust a shot glass in my face. "Mya, what is this?" I ask. Mya smiles & turns away from me to face the guys, "on three, we all do our shots together." She says. I inch closer to her & sniff my shot. Wow is this strong or what. Yup, it is most definitely tequila. "ONE..TWO..THREE..DRINK.." says Mya. We all down our shots & let out some sort of a noise after drinking that straight. JC looks at Mya & says "shouldn't we have a lime or something to suck on? Isn't that tradition for tequila shots?" Mya laughs & turns towards me with a grin that I recognize. She is about to start some trouble. I just know it.

"Shall we dance ladies?" JC asks. Henry smiles at me & holds his beer up to say he is not ready to dance yet. Mya reaches over me, grabs her wristlet & rushes off to the dance floor. I look out at her moving & I watch in envy. She is so beautiful. I wish she knew that. But Mya is not looking for a boyfriend, a fiancé, & definitely not a husband. Not after her breakup with Brody Majors. That was a tragic break up. He was a fool for ending things with her. And boy did he regret it when she broke all of his windows on his pickup truck. She walked away from that truck & locked every emotion or feeling away that night. We never spoke of Brody again. And she has not had a serious relationship since. Brody & Derek did end up becoming good friends. Surprise, surprise. However, once they ended, I didn't let Derek invite Brody to any social gatherings. Mya didn't care either way. But girl code wouldn't allow me to. Not to mention every time I saw his stupid face all I could do was think of how much he hurt my best friend. So, it was best I didn't see him.

Henry looked at me for a bit before breaking the silence. I could feel his eyes on me, but I never took my eyes off Mya. Not only was I mesmerized by her confidence & beauty I was also keeping an eye on her for safety reasons as well. One rule about bars, clubs etc. you never leave a girlfriend alone or take your eyes off of each other or your drinks. It's like I tell Carson, the buddy system. It is key for women on a night out also. It's just proper safety guidelines.

"Would you like to have another drink, or we can dance if you'd like." Henry says.

I smile because I think he is just as nervous as me, maybe even more so. Instantly I feel more comfortable than I have all night. I look over at him "I may not be the best dancer, but I am willing to give it a try." He smiles & takes a breath of relief. He puts his hand out & leads me to the floor. Luckily by the time we make it out there things have slowed down a little. Thank goodness because I would not be able to move to much in these heels or we may have a spill on the dance floor & I do not mean from my drink. We are not quite in a slow dance, but the music has slowed way down. We both kind of stand there & slowly move back & forth. Not touching, however.

He smiles at me & says "Okay, I have a confession to make. I am not a very good dancer either." I laugh & smile. Yes, I am feeling comfortable. I look to my right & see Mya & JC locked into each other, lips almost touching but not quite. She wastes no time, hey I got to give it to the girl. She knows what she wants & she goes for it. I look back at Henry & he is looking at his feet, his cheeks are flushed & he looks embarrassed. I let out a little laugh & put my hands out to grab his. He looks up at me & takes my hands. "Sometimes it is easier to follow the music with a partner if you touch." I speak.

He shrugs & gives me a nervous laugh. "I told you; I am not a good dancer either. But I think you may be a pretty good dancer after all." He says to me.

My eyes flutter quickly & my cheeks grow round from smiling so hard. I have not had butterflies in a long time. But for some reason Henry gives me butterflies by being nervous around me. The song ends & we walk back to our table. Mya & JC have headed back to the bar & Henry & I wait for them to come back. Henry stands there with one hand in his pocket & his other flat on the table. He is still nervous but starting to relax. Mya & JC come back with 4 drinks & 4 more shots of tequila. 2 Corona beers for him & JC, & two vodka tonics for Mya & I. I shake my head at Mya as if to let her know I do not approve of the next round of shots, but she does not seem to care either way. We down our shots & JC asks us if we would like to go out to the beach.

In the back of the lounge are two huge sliding glass doors. The twinkling lights shine from the deck, but not as bright as that gorgeous full moon. We all grab our drinks & follow JC's lead. We walk onto the beach deck & it is an absolute vision. I love the beauty of the beach at night. So serene & peaceful.

Mya & JC walk off the deck & onto the sand under the moonlight. Arms locked together as if they had known each other before tonight. I sit on the sand right by the deck & take these ridiculously tall & painful heels from my feet. I feel relief when my aching toes hit the cool, damp sand.

Henry takes a seat next to me, not too close, but close enough that we can speak quietly.

"The beach is beautiful at night." He says. I never take my eyes off Mya ahead of us who is now kicking water at JC & laughing loudly & crazily. "I love the peace & quiet. It is a nice change of scenery from my day to day life." I say.

Henry sighs. "Tell me about it, different for me to, in a good way. Two kids & just me. This is heaven for me." Says Henry. I glance over to him almost instantly & stare in shock. "You are a single parent with two kids?" I say.

"Widower." He says. "Divorced." I say.

<h1 style="text-align:center">Chapter 6</h1>

I look down at my phone to see an incoming text that I must have missed hours ago when we got here.

"Goodnight mom. Carson is in the boy's camp group Outdoor Avengers. I can keep my phone because I am a camp counselor in training. Love you I will text you tomorrow night." My sweet Clara Paige. She sent that at 9pm on the dot. Her usual lights out time at the camp. I am so proud of her, she is such a great big sister. I am so lucky to have these two amazing humans as my children. I hope they are having the time of their lives.

I look up & see Mya now sitting on the edge of the water laying back, looking up at the moon. I see JC doing the same next to her.

Henry is staring at me; I can see from the corner of my eye. "Sorry, I had a missed text message from my daughter. They are at slumber camp." I say.

Henry smiles. "Slumber camp huh. My two girls have gone with nana & papa for the next two weeks. They enjoy going up to Littleton farm area. That's where my parents live." Henry says.

I look at him with compassionate eyes feeling sorry for his loss. I want to ask what happened, but I would not be so cruel to ask him to relive that type of trauma. "Littleton is a great town. I took my kids horseback riding there many summers. We have stayed at the Cherry Farm INN actually." He looks down the beach & back at me. "The Cherry Farm Inn is a great place to go. Not to far from my parents' farm. They own the Fields Bay Farm. My name is Henry Fields." He says.

I look in awe. Wow, he is basically Littleton Royalty. The Fields own one of the biggest farmlands in all of New England never mind just Littleton. "Wow, that is quite the name around these parts." I say. "Yeah well, don't tell that to JC. He thinks farming is nothing to be proud of. He is more city than country." I laugh because if that doesn't describe Mya – I don't know if this is fate or what but he sounds exactly like Mya.

"What's so funny?" Henry asks.

I smile. "I love watching her. She is so free, it is refreshing." I say.

"Are you two sisters?" he asks. I smile wider & never take my eyes off Mya. "Something like that." I say.

We say goodnight to the guys as we head back towards the front of the hotel. We decided to walk around to the front instead of going back through the lounge. It is a beautiful night. The sand on my feet does feel much better than slipping back into these awful heels to walk through a crowded, dim lit lounge anyways.

Henry is a gentleman, I must admit. I did have fun chatting with him. And it was nice seeing someone else just as awkward as me in a social setting. Mya plants a big kiss on JC as soon as we make our way to the elevator Mya gives me a look as if she is waiting for me to give her the mom approval. I do not. She is coming upstairs with me & she is coming alone. I know where she is going with this kiss so I interrupt by asking the guys if they would like to meet tomorrow for brunch by the pool.

"Sure, I would love that. What time do you think?" says Henry. Before I can respond JC answers for me. "Any time after 12 bro. I am not going to sleep anytime soon." I look over at Mya who has stars in her eyes. "Mya, let's go upstairs so we can get our beauty rest for tomorrow." I say. Mya laughs & pulls away from JC & enters the elevator with me. I immediately push the number 7 on the elevator & the doors begin to close. I look at Henry & shout "Tomorrow, main pool 11am." He smiles once more as the doors close. I look over at Mya who is giving that same devilish grin. "Somebody just made a date for tomorrow, ohhhhhhh. Somebody is going to get some ACTION." She says to me in a very tipsy tone. "Yeah, that's what I am trying to do at 11 am in broad daylight Mya." I say. "Jeesh, live a little will you. Not like it would be the first time you did something in broad daylight." She says giggling.

I turn red. "Mya that was 15 years ago. Must we always re live the past." I say. Mya laughs uncontrollably as the elevator opens on our floor. She tumbles off & rushes off to our room. I grab the key from my clutch & open the door for us. She zooms inside & plops on the bed closest to the AC. Typical Mya. Before I can get undressed & ready for bed she is snoring away. God, I love her, I know one thing for sure. She does know how to pull me back when I am so far deep in a depression. She is probably the only one who can.

<hr>

"Just leave me alone. I don't want to see you or talk to you. EVER AGAIN." I scream at the top of my lungs unknowingly. Everyone on the school campus turns their head to look at the drama unfolding. "Lana, what is the matter with you. Why are you acting like this." Derek yells back. Mya brushes past him & grabs my arm. She looks back at Derek & gives him a dirty look then says "why don't you beat it before I kick your ass in front of the entire school loser." Mya looks back at me & rubs my back as she guides me to the nearest bathroom as the tears begin to spill down my cheeks. I open the bathroom door & throw my bag on the countertop sink & look in the mirror & begin to sob uncontrollably. "Well, I don't need to go to

my next class. I have Ancient History but who really wants to sit through shit that happened hundreds of years ago anyways." Mya says while she stands next to me looking in the mirror also. I try to laugh but I can't catch my breath & it makes me cry even harder. "How could I have been so stupid. How could I have let myself throw everything away Mya. I have a scholarship. What am I going to do now." I say. Mya looks in my eyes in the mirror & says "We are going to do exactly what we want to do as always. Like right now we are leaving school, we are going to get our nails done & then maybe we might get some pizza. And ice cream to but if you want hot fudge, you're paying the extra cost." Mya says in the most serious tone I have ever heard. I look over at her & smile. My tears stop flowing & I say, "Are we going to take my car or yours?"

~~~~~~~~~~~~~~~~~~~~~~~~~~~~~~~~

The sun shining through the tiny space of curtain Mya left open wakes me up. It is 6am. Mya is snoring away & looks so cute & cozy curled up in the middle of her giant bed. I look over at my phone charging next to me. One new text & one missed call. New text from Clara.

"Good morning mom, I am setting up breakfast for the junior campers. I will call you tonight after dinner to check in. Today we are having our swim test to see who can swim out the farthest."

Slumber camp is Clara's favorite place to be. This is her 3rd year going she will be 13 by the end of the summer. Next year she can officially be a jr camp counselor. This year she is in training. Clara is a lot like me. She is caring, nurturing, & motivated to do her share. Carson is just like Derek. He is always the class clown & has no desire to do more than he has to. I love his kind, & sweet soul though. I would like to think he embraced that from me.
~~~~~~~~~~~~~~~~~~~~~~~~~~~~~~~~

I check the missed call & it is from Derek. He called me at 5:30 this morning. He must have been getting up for work. He knows I am an early riser & probably assumed I was awake. He left a message. **"Hey L, I guess you & Mya had a long night. I don't mean to bother you. I hope you're having fun. You deserve it. I will check in later. I lov……..later."**

We have officially been divorced for a whole year. Separated 18 months. And he still says he loves me sometimes. I know he means it in his own way, but not the way I have meant it all these years. I put my phone down & get up to stretch, shower , & search for coffee. I try to move quietly so I don't wake Mya. Then again, a stampede of elephants right now will not wake her.

I step out of the shower & reach for the beautiful fluffy white towel. I dry my hair & body & look at the swimsuits I have packed. I then realize I have packed everything for a weekend away at the grandma convention. All of my swim suits could double for hazmat suits with all the coverage I have going on. I peak around the corner & Mya is still sleeping. I slip on my running shorts & a matching tank, throw my hair into a messy bun & grab my purse. I head out to the little shop I saw in the lobby. I hope it is open by now. I need to do some shopping.

Chapter 7

I step off the elevator & the lobby is quiet. The sunshine coming through the windows is glorious. I see the bright smiles of the hotel staff as I near the front desk.

"Hello, I am in the Rogers room on the seventh floor. What time does the boutique open?" I ask. The pretty red head behind the counter never stops smiling even while she speaks to me. "Yes miss, the store will be opening in about 10 minutes. If you would like some coffee while you wait, it is complimentary in the lounge all morning." She says.

I thanked her & turn to head for some fresh brewed coffee. My favorite. I sure do hope they have some pastries to. I could go for anything blueberry right about now, or banana, or cinnamon, or……… "Lana?" I turn to my right & there is Henry.

"Hi, good morning. What a surprise. I didn't think anyone else was up this early except me." I say.

He nods & shrugs his shoulders "Well I am a farm boy after all." He says. I nod in agreement. "I guess that is true." I say.

He holds the door for me as walk into the lounge which looks awfully different in the morning. All the lights are bright & the back patio doors are wide open & the sunrise from the beach is a beautiful sight bringing warm sunlight into the entirety of the lounge. I see a stand with all different types of coffee urns. Some say decaf, some say different flavors, & some are just hot water. I look down at the table a little & see an assortment of muffins, donuts, bagels, and my all-time favorite, scones.

I adjust my stance so I can slyly walk down to the other end & grab myself a scone without being noticed, although that seems highly unlikely since Henry is right behind me and an older couple. The older woman smiles at me & says good morning. The older gentleman passes me a coffee cup & tells me how good the Maple brew coffee is. As delicious as that sounds, I am a creature of habit. I notice they have decaf coffee which I will mix with original coffee for a half & half effect. I slowly walk down & try to turn my head to see if Henry is watching. He is still trying to decide on a flavor of coffee. I quickly grab a napkin & grab two blueberry scones & put them into my purse. He walks down to my end of the table & grabs two plain donuts & walks by me to grab some napkins.

"Wow, what a spread huh? I guess when you're paying almost a grand to stay just a few nights they should feed you too." Henry says. One grand for just a few nights? How much did Mya spend on this vacation?

"Yeah, I love the assortment." I say. He looks at me & smiles, "Are you going to grab yourself something for now? Or do you plan to eat those purse pastries later at brunch?" he says with a wink.

I am immediately mortified. I am redder than the caution sign in front of the hot water urn. "Oh, I was grabbing some stuff to bring up to Mya, she likes options when she wakes up from a long winters nap. Haha" I say & laugh nervously. Wow, nice one Lana.

He smiles & grabs an extra blueberry scone. "Well, lets get you one too & we can take our stuff out to the beach." He says. I look back at the boutique which is just opening its doors. "Maybe for a few minutes. But won't we be seeing each other at brunch?" I say. He looks back at me while walking towards the back patio. "That is almost four hours from now. Why not get a jump start on some morning energy." He says. I follow behind him quickly as he is now ahead of me. He steps onto the patio with his hand on his hip, his coffee in the other hand & a stack of pastries on top of the mug. He pulls a chair out for me once he has placed his mug onto a small black table on the patio. I sit down & look out at the waves. "It is surely relaxing." I sigh. He looks at me & slides the blueberry scone over to me, "You can say that again." He says.

I thank Henry for the few moments of peace on the beach with coffee. It was nice to sit & chat for a moment. He told me how he loves to have his coffee on his back porch every morning. He lives near the beach himself. But nothing like this one he says.

I scurry through the lounge & rush into the boutique before it gets busy. I look at the tall blonde standing behind the cash register. Her slim waist & large chest tells me she will not be any help in picking a swimsuit for my curvy, robust body. She never looks up from what she is doing but says "Welcome to Beach Babe Boutique." I smile & say "thank you". I walk briskly to the back so I can see if any swimsuits come in size 12 or above. I see a hot pink one piece bathing suit with three open holes traveling down the front. I see a matching hot pink wrap skirt to go with it. I check the sizes in the back of the rack. Size 14. Perfect. I grab the suit & rush to the register, on my way by I spot a cute pair of pink sandals that look rather comfortable. Size 8. My size. What a coincidence. I grab them as well. I walk over the blonde girl & hand her my purchases. She rings them in & still never looks up. "That will be $78.00" she says, again without looking up. I hand her a $100 bill and wait for my change. She hands me a paper bag that says Beach Babe in fancy lettering. I take my bag & change & rush off to the elevator. I head upstairs & prepare to try out the new me. Let's hope I don't regret this.

I open the door to the room & Mya is sprawled across her bed facing me with her phone in her hands. "JC sent me a text saying he wants to get together again tonight too." She says. "You already gave him your number, when did you even have that exchange?" I say. She rolls her eyes & stares at me. "Shopping trip without me?" she says. "And so early too. Beach Babe?" she says reading the bag. I hold the bag behind my back. "Nothing much just some comfy shoes since someone likes to dress me up like a toy doll & watch me break." I say.

She rolls her eyes yet again & rolls onto her back looking up at the ceiling. "I think I might hook up with JC tonight." She says. Now I roll my eyes. "Mya, I think the entire hotel & beach knows you're going to hook up with JC tonight." She laughs & keeps texting on her phone. I look over at the nightstand & notice I left my phone up here the entire time. One new message from a number I have never seen before. **"Brunch 11am, p.s. thanks for the quickie this morning 😊"** it says.

I look over at Mya, then back down at my phone. "Did you seriously give JC my number to give to Henry?" I ask. Mya rolls back over onto her stomach. "Oh please, like I don't know you like him. What's in the bag Lan?" she says. I blush & throw it at her. She sits up on her knees on the bed in excitement & rips the bag open. She pulls out the hot pink suit & begins to whistle. "Okay mamacita, now THIS, THIS is what I am talking about. Now can I please throw every other bathing suit you own away & you can only wear this one for the rest of the trip?" she says sarcastically. I stand & grab the suit from her. "Oh Mya, grow up. I don't even know if it is going to fit." I say annoyed. She jumps up & stretches her arms over her head while yawning. Still in the same romper from last night & her hair is all disheveled. She grabs my hand & drags me over in front of the mirror. "Well, only one way to find out, put it on." She says. I look at myself in the mirror with the pink suit held up to me & smile. Leave it to Mya to give me even the littlest bit of confidence. I slip my running shorts & tank off & begin to wiggle into the suit. My eyes are closed once I get it fully on. I am afraid to look at myself.

But all I can hear is Mya making cat calls at me. I open one eye & I am stunned. "I look…." Before I can finish what I am about to say Mya interjects. "Hot AF, Amazing, Bodacious, like a goddess queen, sexy, delicious, I could go on." She says. "I look GOOD." I say. Mya looks at me in the mirror. "All of the words I just threw at you & you land on "good", really Lana?" she says.

I laugh & smile at my friend's weird way of making me feel comfortable. I do a spin in the mirror in awe of how good this suit really looks on me. It fits amazingly & shows off all the right places. The three holes going down the front mesh to my body so well it looks classy, not trashy. I grabbed the pink wrap skirt & tie it around my waist & slip on the pink sandals. I grab my Dior white sunglasses & let my curls down. Mya turns her head & whistles one more time before going in to shower herself. "Keep it up you bad bitch" she screams from the bathroom. "I knew I would crack your shell back open". She says. I turn my head back to the mirror & smile because she is right. I am already feeling more alive than I have in a while. Maybe this is exactly what I needed after all.

Chapter 8

Mya & I step onto the elevator. & look in the mirror on the doors as they close. Mya has on a metallic black two piece with a very sheer white cover up dress. She is not wearing any shoes & she has a neon green pair of sunglasses on that look incredible on her face. Her hair is tied back in a little ponytail & she has hot pink lipstick on. If I didn't know her I would think she was here for a modeling shoot. Her curvy body & small waist looks amazing in her metallic suit. She is a vision. I look at myself in the mirror & for the first time in a while, I feel like I deserve to stand next to Mya. I feel a little more like myself.

The elevator doors open & Mya brushes past people to get off. She looks back at me & says "people are peopling this morning, lets get to the pool to meet our vacay dates." I look at her with an amused face. "Vacay dates huh? After only one night you are marking your territory pretty fast. That's a new record for you. Usually, you make the guys sweat it out until a night or two before we leave. Are you softening up on me?" I say giggling.

Mya lifts her glasses & gives me a scowl. "Shut up." She says. I laugh as we enter the pool area. I see JC & Henry waving us over to a table they're at with an umbrella right in the middle of the pool patio. Mya rushes towards them & grabs the seat right next to JC. I walk over & Henry pulls out my chair. I must admit he has the manners of a farm boy. "Why thank you." I say. Henry stares at me a little to long, but I am not saying I mind. "Wow, you look, wow." He says. Mya kicks me under the table & licks her lips. I kick her back & look away from her. JC compliments Mya on her pool attire as well. The guys have pre ordered us some mimosas & Mya downs hers & waves the waiter over for another & some extra menus.

The pool is not too busy this time of day. Not many kids here but I do see a few parents down here for an earlier swim with their children. One little boy jumps off the pool stairs & keeps asking his parents to rate his jump. Another little boy throws a water football in & out of the pool with his dad. Watching the kids makes me miss my children. But I just know they're having an amazing time. "And for you miss…." The waiter says to me. I look back to the table away from the pool. "I will start with some avocado toast & a fruit salad" I say. He nods & walks away briskly.

JC & Mya are awfully cozy on their side of the table. There is still plenty of room between Henry & I which I do appreciate. "So what trouble are you ladies getting into tonight? Any plans yet?" JC asks. Mya looks at me & winks. "Well, it all depends on who has the best offer." Mya says sweetly. JC gives her a playful grin & says "How about drinks at Jones's Place & a walk along pier 43 BLVD". Before I can say anything, Henry begins to speak while never taking his eyes off of me. "No, how about appetizers & drinks at Havana Street Lounge & dinner at Le'Cresta." JC turns his head instantly when Henry speaks. "Le'Cresta, what are we rich dude?" Mya rolls her eyes at his comment. "Well at least we know SOMEONE has some taste and can recognize classy girls when he meets them." Says Mya. I look over at Mya, cheeks flushed & roll my eyes.

"I didn't mean it like that girls, but Le'Cresta is Kirkland Beach's only 5 star restaurant." Henry glances over to JC, then back to me. "Would you ladies like to go unless you already had plans of your own. I don't want to intrude or assume." He says. JC looks at Mya who is red with fury looking at her drink menu. "Yeah, would you girls like to go there…. to…. Le'Cresta…. tonight, with us?" JC says while raising an eyebrow. Mya looks over at JC & has a neutral look on her face. This may not be good. She looks back at her menu & says "I suppose so." I look at Henry who is patiently waiting for my answer while sipping his drink. I reply "I think that sounds like fun. We would love to go."

The waiter brings us over our order & we talk amongst ourselves trying to get to know each other better. JC is an accountant with his dad's firm in Boston, his dad has been running his financial company for years & his grandfather before that. And, Henry not only grew up on the farm & works it most of the summer & some of fall. He also has a master's degree in education. His true passion is helping others learn & understand their own passion. He teaches 9th grade economics at Littleton High School. Cue the googly eyes. I think I just found my new crush. Handsome, has & loves children, works on & owns part of a farm in the wealthiest farm town around New England, & teaches kids how to follow their own dreams. Hubba Hubba. Now this is a man. A man I just might take some interest in this week. And by the looks of it he is just as interested in me too. Why? I haven't figured that out yet.

Chapter 9

"I mean, I'm not saying I *don't* want to go, I am just saying, are we sure *these* are the guys we want to go with?" Mya yells from the balcony as I decide what to wear. I turn my head to her direction. "Mya, just because JC thought this place was pricey doesn't mean he's not a total catch. In fact a man who knows how to economize & prioritize his money is someone you *want* in your life." I say. "Especially in your life." I whisper to myself so Mya doesn't hear that part. Mya walks in from the balcony with her hair tied up in a twisted up do. "Listen, a responsible guy blah blah, I have heard it all before. I want to be wined & dined, not financially educated & couped & duped." She says.

I don't take my eyes off my dress I am holding up to my body in the mirror. "Okay, one, if I knew what you were saying I might have a better response, two at some point you may decide you want to settle down, and three what the heck does couped & duped mean?" I say.

Mya laughs & springs onto my bed. "Like thinking you've found a great guy, he wants to take you out, but his idea of a date is the local pancake house with a 2 for one coupon. Duped. Hence, couped & duped." She shares.

Now I turn my head from my reflection in the mirror towards her. I have nothing to say, but I just laugh. "Mya, you truly are one of a kind. I love you." I say.

She smiles & returns the sentiment. "Now stop being mushy & put on something sexy. I know you have a thing for that farm boy. He is pretty good looking. You think little miss Lana piranha might come out to play tonight?" Mya says. I stare at my reflection some more. I have not heard that nickname since …..

~~~~~~

"I don't care what he says. I don't want to speak to him right now. We need our space. Besides I am still PISSED at him. Make sure you say it just like that Mya, I am PISSED at him!" I scream down the hall from my room to the kitchen. Mya laughs loud enough for me to hear 2 rooms down. "And just for the record rock & roll boy; Lana said quote unquote she is PISSED at you. She even asked me to say it in that exact angry tone." I hear her yell. Then she hangs up the phone, grabs the chocolate pudding from the fridge with two spoons & walks back to my bedroom. "Okay, first of all why did you even go out with him, and second of all tell Grams we need to start getting butterscotch pudding again." I slam my closet door holding this red lace top & a pair of black leather pants. Mya's eyes get huge. "Oh so you want to play Lana Piranha & Mya Fire". Mya says in a quirky voice.

~~~~~~

I drop my dress onto the floor. "This is not the dress for tonight, I need something, something, not me. I cannot believe I am about to say this. But let me see what you have for dresses Mya." I say with instant regret. "LANA PIRANAH, let me just say welcome back, you've been missed & you are so going to get lucky tonight." She says with extra enthusiasm.

Chapter 10

I am mixing my water with my extra hydration packet when I hear my phone ding. It must be the kids – I miss them so much. And even though I may actually be having a good time, I miss my babies. I pick my phone up & my heart drops into my stomach when I read my text message.

Exxxxxxxxx – "Hey L, I know it technically isn't our anniversary anymore, or I guess Idk how this all really works. But this is the first year idk what to say. So I guess I will just wish you a happy anniversary or a happy day. Hope you are having fun with Mya. Though, I am sure it is bordering babysitting at this point. Love ya. – D"

I drop my phone onto the bed, fall onto my stomach across Mya's bed. Great, as if I couldn't be anymore pathetic my ex-husband reminded me that it is in fact our 13th wedding anniversary, or would be.

Why would he even send me a text message saying anything. He is the one who ruined everything. He is the one who decided to no longer work at this marriage. No, you know what. Not today, Derek. Not today, I let you have enough of my time & heart & thoughts. Mya brought me here for a reason. I need to, so she says, "get my groove back". I like to think of it as moving on & letting go. And now is my time to do that. Old me would have immediately responded with a socially awkward remark & try to turn it into a humorous thing. But no. It is 3pm and it is almost time for us to start getting ready for our 6pm reservations. Well Mya is napping away on the large chaise lounge on the balcony. I need to wake her up so we can start getting ready. I have my dress Mya gave me hanging on the bathroom door & I am seriously regretting not just wearing my basic black cocktail dress. But no, I let Mya give me a dress to wear tonight. It is an all white dress that is very form fitting. It has beautiful butterfly sleeves & a deep v neck. The skirt is extremely short but the good thing is it has a little slit on the side so that will prevent it from constantly riding up on my thighs.

I finish fluffing up my curls & painting my face with mascara & a wine red lipstick. Then I go get Mya to get up. She rolls off of the chaise lounge & strolls inside the room saying, "Wow, someone looks ready to get some di…"

"Mya Penelope, if you finish that sentence I will refuse to go tonight." I say sternly.

She laughs, but rolls her eyes & says "DINNER Lana, get your mind out of the gutter. Jeesh." I roll my eyes back at her & give her a motherly look. She shrugs & hands me the white dress so she can go into the bathroom for an hour & pamper & prod herself. I am not sure why she does all these things to her face when she is already so naturally pretty. But it makes her happy. Just some lipstick & mascara for me is all I need & want. Besides in this heat, the makeup is bound to drip off of me onto this white dress at some point if I did wear some. Maybe that's why she didn't want to wear white tonight. Makes sense.

45 minutes later Mya swings the bathroom door open, her hair straightening iron in her left hand & a hard seltzer in the other. Where did she even get that from in the bathroom? Goodness gracious. "Okay, I am either going full fledge neon colors tonight, or all black. What do you think Lan?" Mya says. I look over to her holding up a black leather skirt with an adorable black tube top. I think it looks like an outfit you would see on a runway. But then she holds up this bright yellow & orange mini dress & the colors are so vibrant that it is hard not to stare. The dress is one shoulder & the skirt of the dress is surprisingly flowy as opposed to hip hugging. "I

love it. Bright colors look amazing on you." I say to her with a smile on my face.

"I think so too. Besides, it matches my personality tonight. Wild & loud." She says. I laugh & finish slipping into my white dress. Well, I guess this is as good as it is going to get. I brush my bangs out of my face & check my lipstick once more. I slip on Mya's white sparkly sandals she lent me, which are thankfully a wedged heel so I do not have to balance my foot on a tooth pick heel. Mya throws on her dress & pins her hair up in a very stylish 60's do.

We make sure we have everything one last time & head down to the lobby area to wait for the guys. Mya said we should grab a drink to loosen up at the hotel lounge before we go out. That is exactly what we are going to do. As we enter the elevator I feel my phone vibrate in my purse. I look down to a picture of the kids they took all muddy giving me the kiss face. Gosh I miss them.

I feel Mya's eyes on me as I close my phone & slip it back into my purse. "Lana, I say this with love but you are more than a mom you know. You are a sexy woman who is in her prime. Stop comedically acting like somebody's grandma & crying over every picture or text the kids send you." Says Mya with a stern look on her face.

I blink quickly at her because I know she is right. I know most of my time I spend doting over my children & embracing my role in motherhood. But she does make a valid point. I had my kids so young I am only 32 years old. Most mothers I see at the kids school functions are at least 5-10 years older then me if not more. And here I am in my early thirties with two kids and an (EX) husband. I sigh & look at Mya as the elevator door opens. "I know you're right My, but it's hard when all I have ever known is being their mom." I say.

I have not shared with Mya all my pain about the kids getting older & not needing me as much. It adds to the loneliness around the house now. Mya laughs as we step off the elevator. "Be thankful the kids only know the mom side to you, I sure as heck know the OTHER side to you & it sure is wild." Mya says humorously. I shoot her a side eye & roll my eyes making a shut up remark under my breath. She laughs & drags me to the lounge.

"Hi, Mya Rogers, two please." Mya says sweetly to the man in front of the lounge entry. "Table or bar?" he says assertively. I can tell Mya is now flirting by the way she responds. "Depends, what do you suggest for two single gals just looking for a quickie……drink that is." She says flirtatiously.

Good Lord she is at it again. I laugh quietly & I am quite sure my cheeks are turning pink. The guy straightens himself & opens the rope & waves us in "Bar ladies, high top tables are all reserved for tonight." He says in a now softer tone.

Mya winks at him & grabs my hand as we walk inside. I laugh louder when we get past the entrance. "Mya, can you stick to one guy per vacation please." I speak through laughs. Mya rolls her eyes & drags me deeper into the lounge until we reach the large bar in the back. "Two tequila squeelers" Mya tells the bartender. I quickly look at her as if to say WHAT. She ignores me & grabs our drinks & passes me one.

"To tonight" she yells holding her glass up to mine. I hold my drink up while giving her a fierce look of annoyance for having to drink tequila. Mya loves tequila. She sucks her drink down & asks the bartender for another round before I can say anything. I worry we are taking to long and that the guys are searching the lobby for us when I look up & see a familiar face in the crowd. "Mya, is that Ryan Corsin over there?" Ryan Corsin is a long time friend of ours from high school. Well, a long time friend of me & Derek that we once tried to fix Mya up with, that didn't go so well. Ryan is very laid back & Mya is for a lack of better words not. Mya ignores my gesture towards Ryan. She rolls her eyes & downs her next drink. I had always hoped for Mya to settle down & find the guy she deserves & have the happy life I dreamed of having.

"Mya, I am going to go say hi to Ryan, be right back." I yell over the loud music to her. She shoos me away & turns to order a third drink flipping her hair. I smile & walk over to Ryan. "Ryan, Ryan Corsin?" I say, tapping him on the arm. He turns to look at me, beer in his hand. "No shit, Lana Paisley, what the heck are you doing here?" he says. I smile because Ryan seems to be a little bit tipsy. "I am on vacation with Mya." I say.

He looks over to where I am pointing & Mya ever so kindly flips us the bird. He laughs it off & looks back to me. "Wow, Mya huh, long time. Does D know you're on a wild girls trip with that one" he says taking a sip of his beer. Then he quickly shakes his head & puts his beer down realizing what he has said. "Lana, I'm sorry I forgot. What an idiot I am. How are you?" he gives me a sympathetic look. Great, just what I wanted. Pity. "It's okay Ryan, easy mistake. I'm actually fine. And Ironically Derek does know we are here." I tell him.

Ryan shakes his head & laughs "well serves him right then, huh? I hope you know I think he was a fool to let go of a woman like you Lana." He says. I smile & try to brush off his comment. "Thanks Ryan, enjoy your time." I say sweetly. He waves & I walk back to Mya, who is on who knows what number drink. I smile at her & she rolls her eyes. "Do you feel better now that you said hi to that moron?" Mya asks. I laugh & hug her. She looks at me as if I have slapped her in the face. "Don't get all mushy on me Lana Piranha." She says laughing. I smile at her and bump her with my hip. "Thanks for this. I really did need this." I say to her. She looks me up & down & grins….."Yeah, you did. You really did." Mya says sarcastically.

43

Chapter 11

It takes about 25 more minutes before Mya finally agrees to go back out to wait for the guys in the lobby. Henry is already there looking very handsome. JC stumbles behind us out of the lounge waving to us vigorously. "Ladies, wait up. Didn't you hear me calling you in there." JC yells.

I look at Henry & try not to blush at just how handsome he is. I turn to JC & say "um, you couldn't hear much of anything in there. I think they are having some sort of party tonight. The tables are all reserved & the music is louder than last night." I say. Mya brushes past me & wraps her arms around JC & plants a big kiss on him. "I hope you're ready for tonight…" she says with a wink.

Dear Lord, Mya is tipsy & the date has not even begun yet. I instantly turn pink in the cheeks & look at Henry who looks at me as well. "You look absolutely stunning." He says to me. JC interjects before I can respond. "Thanks bro, you do too." says JC with a small laugh. Could him & Mya be any more perfect for each other. I am pretty sure they are both one cocktail away from hitting the sheets & I don't mean in a fun way.

Henry clears his throat & gives a look of annoyance to JC. He reaches for my hand & says "Shall we?" I blush & gladly take his hand. I look over at Mya to make sure she is okay & when I turn around Henry hands me one red rose. A red rose. The flower I have come to loathe.

<div align="center">~~~~~~~~~~~~~~~~~~~~~~~~~~~~</div>

"Another red rose, jeesh could he be trying any harder to get you back. A red rose on your car every single day for 2 weeks straight.

44

"Lana, do you not like roses?" I hear Henry asking. I shake my head apologetically. "No, no roses are lovely flowers. I'm sorry I think I just had a little too much tequila in there. One drink does it." I say. He looks at me with knowing eyes & takes the flower from me. He hands it to JC & motions to give it to Mya. He then grabs my hand & says "forget the rose, the rarest rose is on my arm tonight." Henry takes me by the arm & we walk towards the main entrance/exit. Okay, kind of corny I know but he really is so sweet.

The entire walk there JC & Mya are making googly eyes at each other talking about how hot they both are. I am still feeling a little awkward even with the drink in me. But I am trying to enjoy the night. I am still young, and maybe I still "have it", I tell myself.

We arrive at Le'Cresta & Henry lets the hostess know we are here for the Fields party of 4. We decided to skip appetizers & drinks at Havana Street Lounge since our double dates are already seeing double, if you know what I mean. I could not have picked a better partner for Mya on this little adventure. They sure do know how to keep up with one another.

We are seated only a moment after checking in & we have a great table with a great view of the beach. As the sun sets it looks stunning over the beautiful blue water. I am more of an autumn girl myself, nothing like a good ride through the country with some hot pumpkin coffee on a fall foliage tour. But something about this beautiful sight puts my mind at ease. A beach sunset or sunrise is just good for the soul sometimes, I guess.

Henry & I talk about a lot of different things at the table. He loves art & poetry. Just like me. Occasionally I hear Mya crack up hysterically at something she herself said. Nobody thinks Mya is more hilarious than Mya. I must admit, I love her sense of humor too. She sure knows how to make the conversation light. I stop for a moment to laugh at Mya's boisterous laugh. I let out a soft giggle which makes Henry smile.

JC takes the lead on the conversation of the table. "What brought you ladies to Kirkland Beach for the week?" he says. Before I can answer Mya takes a swig of her drink & says "Lana needed this, messy divorce, plus she needs to get her groove back, & your friend henry is going to do it." With a little giggle & a hiccup she winks at Henry. I am officially mortified. Horrified. Embarrassed beyond recovery. My cheeks are probably as bright as the sun setting in the horizon. "Mya, I think we should use the restroom. I need to speak to you." I say to Mya, dryly. Mya shoots me a look of concern but excuses herself with me. I am too mortified to even look at Henry as I excuse myself from the table. I can hear JC laughing as we walk away.

Once we get to the ladies' room I walk in & whip my head around. "Seriously, can you grow up for five minutes Mya. Does everything have to be a joke & a game. Do you know how embarrassed I am now." I say candidly. Mya looks at me with an overconfident look. "Please Lana, take a joke & stop. You're doing the mom thing again & I am not one of your kids." I look at her with exasperation in my face. "Mya, I wouldn't have to treat you like one of my kids if you did not ACT like one of my kids. Stop drinking & making this night

all about YOU, when clearly there are 3 other people at that table!"
I scold.

Before I can apologize for getting so upset Mya storms out of the
ladies' room without so much as a goodbye. I take a moment to
compose myself & adjust my dress in the mirror. I take a few deep
breaths & check my phone before heading back out.

When I get back to the table it is just Henry. He looks at me with
a look of confusion. "JC & Mya, uh left, I guess it is just us. Is
everything okay?" he says. I sit down & sigh. I put my head in my
hands & shake my head. "Honestly" I say, "No, it is not okay. I am
sorry for what Mya said. I am even more sorry for how I reacted
because clearly, she is upset with me & left bringing your friend
with her." I say softly. He looks away for a moment & then looks
back at me almost checking to see if anyone is listening. "Can I be
honest with you." He says. I look up at him with a nod of approval.
I love honesty. "I was kind of hoping to have some alone time with
you anyways tonight & this really seems more of a one-on-one
restaurant. I am pretty happy to share this night with you & you
alone." He says. "But I am sorry you & Mya seem to be having a
little bit of a disagreement. I hope you know I am not offended or
upset by what she said & you shouldn't be either. I can take a joke
sometimes & don't mind being the butt of one." Henry says starting
to giggle.

I look at him with nothing but a smile & a feeling of comfort. I
was humiliated a few moments ago, not because of what Mya said,
but because I was worried about Henry finding out about why I am
here & what led us to this trip. I figure now or never is the time to
be honest with him.

Chapter 12

I look down at my empty water glass & motion to the waiter. "Vodka soda, with a lime please." I say. Henry looks at my flushed face, then at the waiter. "A glass of Merlot please." He says. I look up at him & back to the waiter. "Scratch the vodka, I'll do the same." I say. The waiter nods & scurries off. I smile & look back down. Henry slides his hands over a top mine. I look up slowly & sigh. "If you want to go back, I can walk you back to the hotel." He says in a disappointed voice.

I smile sweetly & shake my head. "Not a chance Mr. Fields. Didn't you hear? It's mom's night out." I say with a big smile on my face. Henry laughs & nods. "Ah, yes. The big mom & dad night out. I am also on a dad's night out." he says.

I smile. I like Henry. He is a nice, funny, & handsome guy. Plus, he is intelligent, a father, & I think he has his life in order. I mean really, he is my ideal dating pick. Am I even ready to date though? One night out doesn't mean we are dating. Right? Crap. What if he thinks we are dating. I need to tell him the truth about my life right now.

The waiter comes back & leaves our merlot & our dinner menus. I look at the wine, take a big sip & then look at Henry. His smile is contagious. "Henry, I want to thank you for taking me out tonight & being so kind to me the last couple of nights." I say. He actually blushes at my remark. I mean flushed cheeks & nervous smile & all. He speaks in a low voice but responds. "Lana, thank you for coming out with me. I am sure you didn't plan on running around with a random guy on your mom's vacation." I laugh, because truth be told I didn't even plan on a "vacation" at all. But, I am having a good time. So I tell him just that. "Henry, you've been a gentleman. I actually am having a really nice time. And it actually does feel good to have a conversation that doesn't revolve around Star Wars or what the latest teen girl drama is at school." I laugh again. He smiles & nods. "I know that feeling. I have a lot of conversations about dolls & tea parties." I continue to laugh again. We have a lot in common & that makes this "date" a very refreshing one.

We order our food & I glance at my phone hanging out of clutch to see if Mya has text or called. She has not. Neither have the kids come to think of it. I try to refocus my attention to Henry who is telling me about his little girls Maisy & Zoey. They are 8 & 6. His oldest daughter Maisy is a ballerina dancer at Junior Miss Academy for Dance. His youngest Zoey is more of a farm girl. He said she could play in the mud & dirt all day long if they would allow it. She is also adventurous & spunky, so he says.

I share about Clara & Carson, about how Clara is in her teen girl years now that she will be 13 come the end of the summer. And my sweet Carson, though he is 10 years old, his mom is still his best friend. I must admit, I love that for me.

It is a nice wholesome conversation. Henry also shares with me about his late wife Gabriella. She was beautiful & the love of his life. High School sweethearts. She passed away 3 years ago unfortunately in a hit & run. A drunk driver slammed into her on her way from dropping the girls at his parents' house. He told me that he felt guilty for many years because he was grateful his girls were not in the car. My heart breaks for him. What a tragic way to lose your partner & love. Here I am with my sad & pathetic story about a divorce. Makes me feel kind of stupid to share now. But I need to be honest with Henry. I also think it is finally time to be honest with myself. I look at Henry & begin to share some of my woes & I watch his face the entire time. Almost looking for a look of judgement, or apprehension, maybe even a hint of pity. But I see none of that on his face. What I see on his face is just attentive, soft, caring & understanding. He is so focused on what I am saying it is as if not a single other soul exists in this restaurant. His intense look is intoxicating. I could look into his eyes all night & pour my heart out. So, I do just that.

Chapter 13

"You think this is easy for me Derek? I have to tell grams & nonna that I am pregnant! And you won't even come with me to do so. You are nothing but a coward. I wish I never met you. You have ruined my life. I hope you're happy." I say as a slam the phone down. "I HATE HIM." I yell. I look in the mirror, fix my bangs & get out of the car. When I step into the house Mya is already in there eating strawberry shortcake with grams on the couch. I look around to see if Nonna is here too. "Bambina, you are home early." She says to me as Nonna rounds the corner from the kitchen. I can smell the meatballs cooking from the front door. Grams looks up at me knowing the look on my face. I burst into tears & fall into Nonna's arms. "I'm pregnant Nonna. I'm so sorry, I'm pregnant." I scream louder as the tears begin to flow like a waterfall.

<hr>

I look up at Henry to see if he is still listening to my pathetic story. He is. So I go on.

"So about 3 years ago I was decorating the house for Clara's 10th birthday. It was going to be a "Diva" themed birthday. All of her little friends planned to come over dressed in fabulous diva outfits & they would do manicures & have a diva day. Derek was supposed to be getting the cake & he had been gone far to long. I knew Derek was cheating long before this day but I just didn't want to admit it to myself, much less anyone else. Especially him. But today was different. Today was for our daughter & the fact that he used this opportunity to cheat on today of all days was my last straw." I say looking in Henry's eyes. He says nothing but his deep stare tells me exactly what he is thinking. "I got in my car. I asked Mya to stay with the kids & I drove to his office. I knew what I would find. I'm not sure why I went inside, but I did. Derek did a lot of his cheating in his office. It was a private office that he owned & he had a backroom with a couch for when he needed a break. I put the code in & walked back. I found Derek with another mom from the kid's school. I was just completely broken. Not only was he cheating on me but with a woman I had to see every day at our kid's school. And she knew we were married too. Her apologies meant nothing to me while I was raging with anger, screaming & throwing things around. I thought I was going to kill them both. But instead, I raged for a few minutes, adjusted myself, walked out of that office, drove back to my house & threw a birthday party for my daughter. As if none of that happened. When Derek arrived back home with the cake, he asked to speak to me & I did not say one word to him. Mya knew something was going on but she never once pushed me to tell her. She just stayed by my side that day & did any & everything for me. The next day I woke up & filed for divorce. I never spoke of that day again. It was to difficult to relive it all. He moved out about a month later & we lived separately until the divorce was final. We both spent time with the kids as much as possible, but they knew it wasn't the same. Eventually Clara learned the truth, but Carson was still so young & to innocent to understand. And now he lives with his super beautiful, younger girlfriend about 25 minutes away from us. And I am still trying to put my life back together." I sigh & look down. "That is my sad tale." I say with another sigh.

Henry looks at me & takes my hand. "Lana, I am so….." here we go, here comes the pity party & the sympathetic apologies for my pathetic ass. "AMAZED by your strength. I am proud to sit beside such a courageous woman." He says. "And quite frankly, a little bit more intimidated." He adds.

I slowly pull my hand away & look at him with utter shock & confusion. "What?" I say & begin to laugh. "Strength, courage, INTIMIDATED?" I laugh with a ferocious growl that would be more embarrassing if I was not so flabbergasted. "Yeah, it is courageous to stay with a man you know is cheating for years & then blow up on your daughter's birthday & flee with a divorce the next day. I am super amazing." I keep laughing through my words.

He takes my hand again & his eyes beating into me begin to ground me. I take a sip of my wine & look at him while he begins to speak. "I don't see it that way Lana. I see a woman who was so strong she allowed herself to be treated unfairly just to keep her family together. She allowed her children to take priority & precedent to the dark that was happening. I see a woman who is so deserving of love because she gives so much of it, even to those who do not deserve it. A woman who although she was broken, never cracked & held her head high while she raised her children. A woman who finally gained the courage to leave a person who did not deserve her no matter what consequences that brought." He looks down as if he is becoming shy suddenly. "I see nothing but strength in you Lana. You are a force. A beautiful force."

I am utterly shocked. Did he just say that to me. All of it? Or am I drunk on this wine. His smile is so contagious I begin to smile. His eyes are deep & captivating. I find this man absolutely intoxicating. It isn't until I lean over the table & plant a light kiss to his beautifully plump, soft lips, that I realize it is not the alcohol I am drunk on. It is him. Henry Fields. I am drunk on Henry Fields.

<h1 style="text-align:center;">Chapter 14</h1>

Before I know it we are kissing passionately outside of the restaurant. After Henry paid the bill we walked outside to the beach. We made it across the street to the beach & instantly the fire & passion between us ignited. I can't stop kissing Henry & he can't stop kissing me either. It is like tea with honey the way we complement each other. His deep roots & dark eyes that are soulful & wise are making me feel incredibly wild. I don't think I have felt this way since, well I don't know. Next thing I know we are in the sand kissing & touching with the most unbelievable electricity.

Henry pulls back for air & shoots me a sexy grin. "Lana, I am very much enjoying this, but are you sure you want this? I don't want to take anything to far if you are uncomfortable, please tell me." He says.

Good Lord, the fact that he just said that makes me want this passionate evening even more. I nod my head & grab his collar pulling him back into a flaming hot kiss that makes my head spin with desire. His hands begin to wander up & down the frame of my body. His touch is intoxicating, just as his eyes are. Everything about this man is excitable.

Just as I am about to probably freely give this man my body, my phone rings & snaps me out of my heated moment of weakness. I roll onto my side & grab my clutch in the sand ripping my phone out to see if it is one of my kids. It's a number I don't recognize. But Henry does. "That's JC's cell phone" He says. "Why the hell is JC calling me?" I check my phone to see if I have any other texts or calls. Nothing. Next thing Henry's phone begins to ring. He answers on the second ring "Yeah" he says in a breathy tone. Henry looks in my eyes in a serious way.

He says "be right there" to JC. I look at him with concern. "You're friend Mya ran off & JC can't find her. She left her phone in the room & took off." He says. I jump to my feet & grab my clutch. "We need to go, now!" I shout.

Chapter 15

I run so fast back to the hotel I nearly leave a cloud of smoke behind me. I have my shoes in one hand & my clutch in the other. Henry trails a little behind me & I am hoping it is just to get a good view of me from behind. Although I am sure I look anything but sexy right now as I run at a speed I have not ran in years & my white dress is probably ripping at the seams over my extra round arse.

Finally I see the hotel in my line of sight. I am nearly out of breath & I am probably covered in sweat but we made it. I also think I broke a bone in my inner thigh from over use but, I am just going to have to deal with it later & send Mya any medical bills.

Bending over & holding my knees I try to catch my breath when I see JC walk up to us in the lobby. He reminds me so much of Mya because he is wasted right now & I smell pot. So not only is he drunk off his ass I am pretty sure he is equally stoned out of his mind. Now I am furious. "What….. the ……. hell….. happened ….. JC. Where did Mya go? Did you do something to her. I swear to God if you hurt her or touched her I will be the scariest person you ever met!" I yell to him while still catching my breath.

Henry is by my side to help me right myself & stand straight. "Yeah, JC what the hell is going on man, how do you just loose a girl? What happened?" he says.

JC shakes his head & steps back a little with his hands up & away from me. "Hey listen, I didn't do anything to her. We came back to the room, things got a little heated. She asked if I had any pot, I rolled a joint we smoked on the balcony & I thought she went in to use the bathroom. When I came back in she was gone. I tried calling her but her phone was on the bathroom sink." He says shakily.

I look at Henry & then at JC. I shake my head & start to grow even more angry. "So let me get this straight, you brought my friend back to the room to have sex with her, got her stoned & somehow lost a 31-year-old woman!?" I scream at him. He looks down at the floor so he doesn't need to make eye contact with me. I am pretty sure JC is afraid of me. He is doing what Carson does when I yell at him for not doing his homework. JC avoids all eye contact & quietly says "I didn't suggest we come back to the room, Mya did." He said.

I roll my eyes because he is probably telling the truth if I know Mya. I drop my head & cover my face with my hand. I take a deep breath & let out a huge sigh. I plop down on the couch in the lobby & begin to think. Think where the hell could Mya go on this beach. Anywhere really. I think back to places we might have passed on the sprint back to the hotel. Nothing comes to mind because I was so focused on getting here I didn't check my surroundings. Then I jump up & run to the elevator. The guys look at me in shock. I look over to them & say "are you two coming or are you just going to stand around looking at me?" They follow me to the elevator & as it opens I hit the top floor. 21. I know we can get roof access up here.

We get to the 21st floor after which seems like an hour ride up. I swing open the door that says "Roof Access". Only to be stopped by a second door that requires key access. "Shit." I whisper. The guys look at the door & look at me. "I am going to do something & I don't want any judgement." I say.

When Mya & I were in school together we used to sneak out through the gym doors & come back in through the lunchroom doors. They were always locked from the outside & required the same key card access. Mya & I learned a trick to getting around key card doors & I am pretty sure she is up here on this roof once I see the type of lock it is. I swipe my credit card down the key reader & immediately swipe another card just after that. It throws of the card reader long enough to punch in a code manually. I type in the key access code that is on the key code to the pool. I assume the hotel only uses one key code. The door instantly flashes green & I open it up. I walk up the stairs faster then ever. I hear henry behind me talking to JC. "You didn't think to check the roof?" he whispers to him. JC shakes his head & laughs loudly, I might add & replies; "Bro, why would anyone willingly come to the roof on this high ass building." I look back & snicker at him "Someone who IS HIGH …. You idiot." Henry shoots me the biggest grin & elbows JC. I know he is not finding the humor in the situation but more so finding the humor in my inability to be scary. Well for some people anyways. I swing open the sliding door on the roof & step out. SHIT. We are really high up & it hasn't hit me until just now. I see the entire beach from up here. There is nothing up here but tubes & what looks like vents. I see two benches on the other side of the roof overlooking the water. I see a pair of heels & run towards the bench. Mya's shoes are here… but no Mya. So she was here. I look around & look around but the roof is only so big. She is not up here. But she was. So where the hell did she go?

I stand near the edge of the roof so I can get a good look at the entire beach, although its dark at this point & I am not wearing my glasses so I can't see very well. When all of a sudden I hear Henry say "over there". I run towards him & he is pointing down at the beach. A girl wearing absolutely nothing is wading into the water with her hands above her head like she is about to swan dive into shark infested waters in the dark of night. I screech & turn on my heels to head back for the door. She is on the private side of the beach connected only to this hotel. I run down the stairs at a speed I wasn't even running on my way up. I know Mya is a grown woman & can take care of herself but she has been drinking, she is upset with me & now she is also high. I need to get to her before she does something stupid. Like I don't know swim in shark infested waters in the dead of night. Naked.

I get to the bottom of the steps & bypass the elevator. I take the stairs back down & I hear Henry yelling to me to take the elevator. I ignore every word he is saying. I want to get to the beach & I can run down 21 flights of stairs faster then the elevator will take me stopping at a bunch of floors on the way. I am so out of breath I think I have used up every last drop of oxygen in my body. I see stairwell 10 on the wall. 10 more flights to go & I am ready to pass out. I finally reach the bottom & swing the back exit door open & fall into the sand. I have no time to catch my breathe. At this point I dropped my shoes because they were weighing me down. Remind me to make Mya get those for me before we go home. I make a mental note for myself. I sprint along the beach calling her name & at some point the guys wind up behind me. I see Mya floating on her back looking up at the sky in the water. She doesn't hear me yet but I am getting closer. The sand feels cool on my hot body that is drenched in sweat. I get halfway to the water & I scream "MYAAAAAAA". Finally she looks over at me in the most nonchalant way.

Oh, when I get to her I may just drown her myself & feed her to the sharks. She looks away & back up to the sky. I am not sure I care at this point so I am wading into the wader in her white dress with my clutch in hand. I realize my phone is in here so I turn to Henry & JC who are just catching up & yell "catch!" as I throw my bag to him. I look down at Mya in the water. She has glossy eyes like she has been crying. But I know Mya & Mya does not cry. She is just really stoned.

Chapter 16

Do you want to tell me what the fuck you're doing out here Mya? I say sarcastically to her. Because I honestly don't care why she is out here she just needs to get out of this water.

Mya rolls her eyes & shoots me a quick glance." Mama Lana to the rescue." She says with a little giggle at the end of her words. Yeah, she is stoned. "Mya, what are you doing in the water in the pitch black. There are sharks & everything else out here. Not to mention you scared JC & me to death. Also, you really know how to put a stop to a fun evening for me don't you. She lifts her head lightly at this point & glances past me to JC with another eye roll she puts her head back down in the water. "A girl can't go for a swim & be one with nature." She says to me.

"Mya what is going on….. look I'm sorry I yelled at you back at Le'Cresta but why are you acting so childish." She snaps her head out of the water & stands. Her wet, naked body glistening under the stars & moonlight. I look down & think of Henry staring at Mya's beauty. Mya looks at me & begins to get frustrated & yells to me. "Childish? Childish? Lana YOU ARE NOT MY MOTHER. STOP ACTING LIKE EVERYONES MOTHER. Do you even know why I really brought you here. DO you even know?" she says still yelling.

I look at her my eyes glaze over because I want to cry right now. For many reasons. One my best friend & practically sister is screaming at me in front of these two guys we barely know. I am exhausted from running all over being worried about her. And I am standing up to my waist in water while she stands facing the men in her naked beauty.

"Mya, I am not trying to be your mother. But when you do things like this the people who love & care about you worry." I say softly.

She laughs & nods in JC's direction. "Who him? I barley know him, he is just some guy" she says harshly. I am embarrassed for him.

I look at her with bewilderment. I love her to death but she needs to get it together. "No Mya, ME. For Pete sake ME!" I shout.

She looks at me & yet again rolls her eyes. I could smack her right now if she rolls those eyes one more time. Henry yells to me from the shore & waves a towel in his hand. The boys must have grabbed towels when they got to the lobby. I wade in toward him & grab a towel. I say thanks over my shoulder & wade back in. "Here, wrap yourself up in this & lets go to shore before a shark eats us." I say jokingly. Although not really because it's a valid fear.

She grabs the towel from me & wraps it around her chest & shoulders. Not yet ready to cover her full body so the towel doesn't get wet.

"I'm sorry if I worried you. But I don't know why he even called you." she says quietly.

I grab her arm & hold her as we walk in. Once I am close enough to her I can hear her teeth chattering from the cold water.

"It's okay. We will talk about it later. I am just glad you're ok." I say.

Chapter 17

Mya slips her dress back on after drying off properly. Her & JC are chatting to the side. Really Mya is scolding him for calling me. I look over & see Henry sitting by the water feet in sand. I walked over to him swiftly.

"So, I guess this wasn't the night you had in mind. Was it?" I say shrugging my shoulders.

"Not really, but I will take any night you give me to get to know you better." He says with a sweet smile on.

"Yeah, well are you sure you still want to get to know me better? After all I have that crazy other half over there." I giggle & nod my head over to Mya. She is now watching me from a few feet away.

Henry looks over to Mya & JC & then back to me. "If you want to have the rest of the night with Mya, I understand. But if you are free in the morning, I would like to try to have a do-over of tonight. Can I take you somewhere?" he says, while standing.

I look over my shoulder at Mya & JC who are still talking amongst themselves. And back to Henry who is now standing & staring right in my eyes. "Okay, I would like a do over. I think we can probably do better than tonight." I laugh as I speak thinking of the disaster this night turned into.

"Really?!? Ok great. Meet me in the lobby around 8am?" He says in an excited tone.

He gives me a small peck on the lips & I thank him for being such a gentleman & a great FBI agent in helping me find Mya. Then we part ways.

Chapter 18

I grab Mya's arm & we begin to walk into the lobby. She tells me she wants to go spend some time with JC tonight alone. I know what that means. Apparently, the evening has not ended for them but it has for me. I tell Mya I would like if she came upstairs with me to talk before, she goes to spend the night with JC. She agrees & we separate from the guys & head upstairs.

"You know I thought you were trying to drown yourself or something crazy like that. From the roof top you looked like you were about to jump in & let the ocean take you away." I tell her.

"Yeah, I don't think you have to worry about me trying to off myself anytime soon. I'm far to young & beautiful to die now Lana. Besides I still have a lot more places to see & people to do." She says as she erupts out into laughter.

I smile at her yet I am still frustrated with her. I know Mya is right that sometimes I don't always let myself live like a younger version of myself would. I am only 32 & sometimes I act like I am 52. I think I have aged myself over the years to protect myself. From what, that I don't know.

"What were you doing in the water anyways? Felt like going for a swim while under the influence in the dead of night." I say bluntly.

She looks at me & continues to laugh. "One day Lana you're going to realize life isn't always so serious. You don't always need an explanation for things & everything doesn't have to be planned out to your liking. Spontaneity is a beautiful thing when you experience it. Try it sometime."

I look closely at her. She's right. I won't tell her that. But she is. She is absolutely right. I look at her with a deep stare & finally let out a great big sigh & hug her. "I know you don't need me to mother you, but sometimes I like to. I love you Mya. You're one of the most important people in my life next to the kids. If anything ever happened to you I'd be lost without you. I need to lighten up. I get it. But you need to tone it down. If I promise for the rest of the vacation to lighten up….will you tone it down a little?" I say smiling.

She rolls her eyes but with a smile on her face. "I'll see what I can do. You big baby." She says giggling again.

I hug Mya & say goodnight at she rushes off to meet JC for the remainder of the evening. I know she is wild & free at heart. I look in the mirror as I wipe my face clean from tonight's make up. I pull my hair into a messy bun & go plop down on the bed. I grab the tv remote & my phone to plug it in. 11pm on what would be my former 13 year wedding anniversary. I never responded to Derek. He saw I left him on read. Good. I can't stand him. I know we remained cordial for the kids but for this entire year he has played head games with me. He loves me, he loves me not, he loves me, he loves me not. Although I think its safe to say he loves me not since he is living with another woman. Good luck to her. I scroll through my messages when I see a random number I haven't yet saved.

It says, **"Brunch 11am, p.s. thanks for the quickie this morning ☺".**

I looked at the number & realize this is Henry. I immediately updated the number to his now saved contact. "Henry Fields". I don't know why but I decided to send him a message.

"Hi Henry. It's Lana. I'm sure you know that though since you texted me earlier. Haha. Well, I just want to say I really

enjoyed the little alone time we did have tonight & I was wondering if you wanted to grab one more drink at the lounge downstairs. Let me know. If not that's totally ok. I'm sure you're exhausted what with our adventurous night. Well, if you want to though. I'm free. I mean… sorry if you're sleeping. I'm terrible at this & way out of practice. If you don't answer I understand."

Shit. Did I just hit send. Oh dear Lord. This man probably thinks I'm a blubbering idiot. Lana why do you suck at this & why didn't you do this while Mya was still here so she could read & edit this for you.

I wait a couple minutes & sigh. Locking my phone & plugging it in. Great. Now not only does he think I'm a boring old mom with a wild friend, he also thinks I am an uneducated idiot for not being able to ask a simple question. I pull the pillow over my face & softly yell into it. Maybe I am destined to be alone. Do I even want to be with someone? I do everything by myself & don't need anyone messing that up for me. I mean sure he is good looking, & sweet, & funny, & he himself is a dad…… but no. I am fine by myself. Besides I don't want anyone to ever hurt me again. I do better alone. I mean let's face it my track record for dating cheaters goes way back. The mom from the school was not the first or only woman he cheated with.

"So, what Derek? You think calling my house every night & flowers are going to fix the fact that you were kissing& gosh knows what else with Vicky Sinclair? Let me guess you're SORRY. Well I'm sorry to Derek. Sorry I ever met you. Sorry I ever got pregnant by you & sorry I love you!"

There is a soft knock at my door. I look up it is 11:30 at night. What the heck. Who could it be. I've seen stuff like this in movies. The hotel staff or who you think is hotel staff picks single women to pry on. They lure them out into the hallway to get kidnapped for sex slavery. Yeah, I am not falling for it. I will not answer that door. Mya has a key so it can't be her. Plus, she would not be knocking softly if it was her. I snuggle down into the covers & listen as the knock persists. Still soft.

I finally get up the courage to say "Who is there? Hello?" when I hear the voice of exactly who I wanted to.

<h1 style="text-align:center">Chapter 19</h1>

Henry Fields is at my hotel room door. I jump up & let my hair down & wiggle out of my hotel bathrobe. I take the eye patches off my under eyes & adjust myself a little in the mirror. Wishing I brought anything to sleep in other then these flowered shorts & camisole set. Gosh Lana act your age! Act any age younger than what you're acting.

I walk briskly to the door & swing it open. Not gracefully I might add as I stub my toe on the door as I do so. "owh…Henry. Hi what's up?" I say gritting through a sharp pain radiating my pinky toe with my hand on my hip trying to be sultry & failing miserably.

He smiles & looks down at my toe which is curled up like a dying snail with salt on it. "Are you okay? That had to have hurt." He says.

No shit. It killed worse then a stupid little papercut that makes you see your life flash before your eyes. "No, I'm fine. Come on in. What brings you up here?" I say, turning on a curled toe and guiding him in the room.

He reaches out his arm for mine & motions for me to grab hold of it. I assume since I am struggling, he wants to help me not make a fool of myself. To late Lana. To late. We walk out to the balcony & sit on the nice lounge set out there.

"You texted me. Unless you didn't mean to send it to me?" he said, trying not laugh.

Lana you're a total moron. Why are you this way. I think to myself while trying to find the words to say to save myself even more embarrassment.

"No, I did mean that for you. I'm sorry if the text was to forward or to indecipherable." I say beginning to turn pink in the cheeks.

"I just thought maybe since JC was busy tonight with Mya you might want to get a drink downstairs before last call at 1am. But I get it it's late. I am not even dressed. It was silly." I voice.

He looks at me with those handsome eyes & that amazing smile of his. It's not until now that we are in the moonlight with complete silence that I notice he has a hint of green in his brown eyes. I am practically drooling at the sight of him when he begins to speak & I snap myself out of ogling this man.

"Lana, I know this is probably all new for you. Starting over with other men. But please stop apologizing for just being yourself. That's honestly one of the things I really like about you. If it makes you feel better this is all new to me too. Gabby died three years ago but I have not dated anyone since. I did have one date with one of the girls' former teachers but that was more of a blind date thing & I wasn't ready." He says with those gorgeous eyes still on me.

"I would love to have a drink with you. I would love to just sit here with you & drink nothing. I just want to get to know you. More & more, as much as you will divulge. I like you Lana. A lot." He says & I nearly jump on his lap & start kissing him passionately. Ok, so maybe I do need a man. Clearly my body sure thinks so. Well remind me to have a conversation with my body when we get home. If she wants a man she better start cooperating with me.

I smile at him so big that it may be bordering a psychotic smile. "I like you too. I was trying to be "spontaneous" like Mya said. I just thought we could have a night cap."

He laughs & shakes his head "Please don't take any advice from Mya. There is a reason JC & I have different taste in women."

I laugh out loud at that. "Ok, so if you give me 5 minutes I will slip into a dress & we can go down & get a drink." I say standing.

"Let me order a bottle of champagne & have them send it up. We can sit out here on the balcony. It is a gorgeous night & quite frankly I like the quiet & you don't have to change." He says & I have never felt more at home.

Chapter 20

My heart is racing. I want to runaway but I also want to run towards him. I wish I knew what the right decision was. I guess there is no "right" decision at this point. Nonna Razza & Grandma Harper give me a look that tells me I should go to him. They think we need to kiss & make up. I think I want to punch him in the face & throw up. Derek walks towards me slowly with his parents. Great. His mom already dislikes me. "Ms. Razza, Ms. Harper, Lana...." Says Mr. Paisely. Yep, I want to runaway now. Derek grabs my hand & kneels without a blink of an eye..... in front of everyone.... His parents, my nonna & grams..... Mya who is peeking out the window of the living room... "Lana Edith Harper ...... will you marry me?" says Derek shakily. I look down at him & the small diamond ring he is placing on my finger, then over my shoulders at Nonna & Grams, & back to Derek.... ".....I, sure, I.....yes, yes I will". I say extremely unsure.

The room service arrives with a bottle of champagne & a fruit bowl. I do love a good fruit bowl. Let me make a mental note to grab those bananas & apples for the morning. You can never have enough fresh fruit around. I smile sweetly at Henry & grab the glass of champagne hands me.

"You look lovely in the moonlight Lana." Henry tells me as he takes a sip of his champagne.

I blush & giggle. I have no idea why but I suddenly feel like a teenager again. Sipping champagne late at night on the balcony under the moonlight with a man I don't know but good Lord is he fine.

"So, I know this night has been a little weird, but I would love to know more about you Lana." Says Henry. "In fact I feel like I need to know every single thing there is to know about you."

I turn my head while sipping my beverage. What the heck more could he want to know. I spilled my guts at dinner about my pathetic divorce.

"Well," I say clearing my throat…. "what would you like to know exactly?" I say.

""Anything you want to share really… I am in awe of you." He says.

Okay, he sure is a smooth operator. Is it getting hot out here or is it him?

"Well, I grew up not to far from here. My parents split up when I was pretty young. Both of my grandmothers raised me when I refused to choose between my parents. My dad was going to be my choice since my mom was not the worlds best at being a mom but she tried I guess. My dad had a softer approach to parenting than her. My Grandma Harper lived a few streets over & I spent most of my time there with her growing up so eventually I kind of just went there & never left one day. And then my Nonna Rozza my mothers mom moved in with us & they raised me together. They have both passed away now unfortunately. I miss them so much every day. They were my best friends. They took the best care of me & my kids. I am honestly not sure how I am surviving without them. I guess with Mya's help. If it wasn't for her I am not sure what I would do. I have a younger sister who decided to stay with my dad & she is good, but we are not as close anymore. She is in college & I couldn't be prouder, but we just are living two different lives." I sip my champagne again & take a big breath.

"I am sorry about your parents." He says. "But it sounds like you had a great time with your grandmothers."

"I did. Nonna Razza was pretty strict growing up but once I got a little older she calmed down & when I got pregnant with Clara in my first year of college I thought she would be more angry but she was so supportive. Grams too." I say.

We talk some more & share a little more. Henry tells me all about his younger life & growing up on the farm. His grandparents & his first job on the farm. I share some of my stories about the kids & some adventures Mya & I had in our younger years as well. When I realize it is just about 2am. We talked for almost two hours. I yawn & try to stand on my now sleepy legs. I stretch & shake my legs a little to wake them up. Henry stands with me holding his hand out to help steady me. His eyes tell me he wants to kiss me, but being the gentleman, he is he instead asks me if I am cold & would like to go inside. I nod & follow him inside.

As we walk in the room & Henry closes the sliding door behind us I begin to think of what Mya said about me being an old lady basically & letting myself go. I know Henry is to much of a gentleman to make the first move, so I turn quickly & gaze into his eyes, & then I plant a kiss on his soft lips. I feel like a fire is burning inside of me. I was so ready for us to take things further on the beach but now that we are back in my room I am burning with desire, but also trembling with fear. His hands begin to tangle in my hair as he tilts my head back to kiss me deeper & more passionately. I would be lying if I said this was not the most action I have had in months, years really.

As we are entangled in a fiery, passionate kiss I begin to think of what this could potentially do if we move further. What if he seems like a nice guy but really this is all an act just to get me to bed. And it is working because I am so desperate for someone's touch & attention. I begin to sweat with anxiety & I shake a little as I pull back. Henry pulls away & grabs my hand. "The last thing I want is for you to do something you are not ready for. I can sense this isn't the right time for this. So I am going to say goodnight to you & head out." He says in the most sexy deep voice I've ever heard.

I sigh & sit on the edge of the bed. I drop my head into my hands & start to giggle. Henry is staring at me like I am an absolute nut job now. I can't help but laugh uncontrollably now.

"Sit down Henry." I say as I pat the seat next to me on the bed. "You are such a gentleman. I want to kiss you & go further with you. I darn right act out all the fresh little thoughts in my head with you." I say in utter disbelief that I just spoke those words. But somehow have zero regret about it. "But I am afraid that if we do this tonight. If we you know, go all the way. What will it mean for the morning. Will this entire chemistry disappear? Will we know longer be in this little fantasy world of butterflies & sweet thoughts?" I ask.

Henry grabs my hand again & tilts my head to look at him. "You have nothing to worry about there. I do not do things like that Lana. I am sure you have had experiences before where maybe you encountered some jerks but I am not a jerk. And if you need time to see that & learn that then we have no need to move further tonight. There is plenty of time for us to get to know each other more & learn these things. I have full intentions of sticking around Lana, I am very interested in you. More than you probably realize. You are a complete catch." He says.

I can't help but blush & laugh again. "Henry, the last man I've been with was my ex-husband. Before that I only had one other partner & that was our senior year of high school when Derrick & I broke up for a few months. Otherwise, that's the only experience I have ever had. I am not as experienced as you think. Even for a 32-year-old woman. I am sorry." I say still blushing.

I feel like Henry's eyes are blazing through my soul now. I shut my eyes to give myself a moment of relieve when I feel his hand on my cheek. God why does this man have such sexy hands & who the heck does he think he is placing them on me when I am feeling already weak to his touch.

"Lana, whatever pace you need to go at is fine with me. I am also not the experienced man you think I am. I told you about Gabriella. I married my high school sweetheart. What do you want? What does Lana want? I want to show you that all you need to do is ask & you will be given what you want. You deserve a man to show you how special you are." He says to me.

Well, that sure messed me up. I am now seeing through blurry vision as my eyes begin to water. I place my hand on top of his on my cheek. I lean in to kiss him again. I feel the softness of his lips as he kisses me back. I look at him & say "I want to feel this again. I want to feel the passion, the desire, the fire. I feel this with you. And I don't want it to end. Not now." I say as I lean in & kiss him deeper. I climb into his lap as we kiss passionately in a world of our own that feels like a twirling merry go round in my mind as I am spinning round & round with stars & wonder in my eyes.

I begin to unbutton Henry's shirt & I do not stop kissing him the entire time. God, I could kiss this man forever. I know this is crazy. We just met yesterday. How can I be so wild for someone I barely know. But I also feel like I do know him. I have dreamt of a man like him.

I begin to take control & damn if it doesn't feel amazing. Our heated make out session somehow makes it from a seated position to us entangled in each other laying on the bed. We are both half dressed & it gets pretty wild when my phone dings. And then dings again. I don't want to stop to check my phone, but I think about the kids & what if it may be one of them. I roll away & break our locked lips to grab my phone on the nightstand. Who could be texting me at almost 3am. I nearly faint when I see the message.

"Hey L. I know you are probably sound asleep. But yesterday being the 13th anniversary of us, well it really makes me think about us. What we were, what we could have been. What we should have been. I have no one to blame but myself for my own actions, I know this. I know we were a family until I ruined it. You were the best thing to ever happen to me. Idk what I am doing but I just hope maybe we can talk. No matter the outcome just know I still love you." -D

"Everything okay?" asks Henry.

I drop my phone & suddenly feel nauseous. I am not the least bit surprised Derek wants to play games with my head. He knows I am out with Mya for the week. He doesn't mean this. Does he? He is living with his younger girlfriend of months. What would suddenly change his mind now? I feel like the room is spinning & it is not from the champagne. I look at Henry who looks devilishly handsome in this evening lighting. I give half a smile & sit up.

"Maybe I need a glass of water & a moment to think." I say flustered. Henry, being the complete gentleman he is, which is starting to drive me mad that he is so perfect, stands & begins to walk to the mini fridge for a cold water for me. My mind is hurting from what I just read & from staring at my one-way ticket to ecstasy right about now.

"Thanks." I say as I take the water from him. "I just need a minute." I say as I go to stand & adjust what little clothing I have on suddenly feeling very aware of my imperfect body. As if Henry reads my mind he hands me the sweater hanging on the back of the chair near him.

"Lana, do you want me to go?" he asks in a defeated voice.

"No, I….no, I just… I got a text from my ex-husband. I think he has a way of knowing when my heart has started to heal. He likes to shatter the pieces all over again." I say as I stand with my sweater wrapped around my body in a tight hug.

Henry stands in front of me & kisses my cheek gently. "I understand. I would never pressure you or want you to feel you have to do something. I am not going anywhere. We have plenty of time for this." He says giving me a smile & walking towards the door.

"How about brunch in a bit?" he says.

I smiled to myself & look over at him. What am I doing? Derek is not going to take this from me too!

I throw my sweater off my shoulders & leap into Henry's arms. Wrapping my legs around his waist. Praying the whole time that I am not to heavy for him or crushing his internal organs with my massive thighs. I kiss him vigorously & motion us back to the bed.

"Lana, are you sure?" he says.

"Henry, kiss me & shut up." I say as I put my finger to my lips motioning for him to quiet. I must admit Mya has rubbed off on me because this side of dominance I am showing is all her. Never in a million years have I been this aggressive.

Henry throws me back on the bed & we spend a little more time kissing before all the clothing is officially gone. His heated, perfect body feels incredible against mine. And my former insecurities are out the window as I encourage his hands to explore my nude curves. I have not felt so strongly about something in my entire life. And in this moment I know. I want Henry Fields to make love to me. And not just sweet loving romantic love either. I wouldn't mind if he excuse my French banged me like a drum. This is the kind of fire I have been craving. This is who I want to be. Fearless. Like Mya.

<h1 style="text-align:center">Chapter 21</h1>

I wake up to the sound of my phone ringing over & over again. I look over to see 3 missed calls. All from Mya. When I see the time stamp on my phone I see it is almost 10:30 am. I never sleep this late. I jump up out of bed only to realize I am completely naked. And there is a guest in my bed. I look down to see Henry who is still sound asleep. I don't blame him as we were up until the early hours of this morning having by far the best sex of my life. God is that man perfect or what. Also, I am officially a huge slut. But I am not even upset about it. I slept with someone on the first date. Go me. I slip into the white robe on Mya's bed & sneak out to the balcony with my phone. I close the sliding door as quietly as possible & dial Mya's number back.

"Well it's about damn time. What the heck where you doing I have been calling & calling. JC & I are heading down to brunch. He has been trying to call Henry too but no answer. We wanted you guys want to meet us down there." She says.

I start to blush & giggle a bit as I slyly say "Henry is still sleeping, he is with me."

"Lana Edith Harper…. Are you saying what I think you are saying?" Mya yells.

"I don't know what you're talking about My, but if it's about me knocking boots with Henry Fields then YES!!!!!!!" I squeal in a very hushed tone. As I do a little bouncy jig as if she can see me.

"Good girl. Now you are a slut just like me." She says as she bursts into hysterical laughter.

"Yeah, yeah." I say smilingly.

"I will get Henry up & we can meet you guys by the pool for brunch in about half hour, 45 minutes. Sound good?" I ask.

"See you there, you big skank." She says jokingly hanging up immediately so I cannot respond back to her.

I slip back inside quietly when I see movement in the bed. I watch as Henry rolls over & stares at me with the most handsome morning daze I've ever seen. "Hi." I say.

"Hi." He says back.

"Did you sleep well?" he asks me.

"I did, well whatever sleep I got anyways." I respond giggling.

Henry smiles at me. I smile back. "Our pals called us & want to meet at the pool for brunch. Half hour enough time for you to get ready?" I ask.

"Yeah, let me just head to my room to get some fresh clothes on." He tells me.

He gets up & throws his clothes on & rushes off to change leaving me with a small peck on the lips & a squeeze of the hand.

Well, that felt very one night ish. I hope my fears are not coming true. I really like Henry. I like him so much I even slept with him on the first date. So very unlike me, more like Mya but…I wanted him to know that I am all in. Was it too soon like I had thought? Is this going to be just a fling. I am at the beach, people who come to the beach have flings all the time. Is that what this is? "Lana stop being crazy" I tell myself. I head to the bathroom to start to get ready, and I am not even going to address the text from Derrick. At least not until I get back with Mya. She will shut that down quickly. Even if I don't.

A little later:

"Lana!" Henry calls from the lobby as I step off the elevator. I decided to go a little more modest with my all black one piece & a pair of high waisted jean shorts & some mom/nursing shoes as Mya calls them. A.K.A my white crocs. I smile & lift my sunglasses from my face. "Hey! Long time no see stranger." I say with a wink. Then I instantly regret it. What a cornball I am. Jeesh talk about out of the game. Is flirting even required once you've done the deed? I sure hope not because I suck at it.

We stride into the pool area & head to the outdoor dining patio. Maya & JC are already sitting at a table for 4. Maya waves to us & has that immature smile on her face. I could see it from the elevator. That fresh little smirk she is wearing is louder than her.

"Hi lovers, how was last night? What's the latest scandal?" Maya says in a comedic tone.

"Morning all." JC says with his sunglasses on.

Someone looks very hungover.

"Maya, JC. Morning." Henry says.

"Maya, let's keep the raunchy remarks to ourselves this morning." I say sweetly & quietly as I take a seat next to my best friend.

The waiter comes to our table to get drink orders for myself & Henry.

"Just a water for me, please." I say.

"Tea, black with one sugar please." Henry says.

"So nobody is having bloody Mary's or morning mimosas with us?" Mya giggles while looking at JC.

"This is my hangover cure, a bloody Mary with a beer chaser." JC groans out while keeping his head down.

I laugh & smile at Henry who isn't even paying attention. In fact, he looks more nervous then when we first met.

I reach for his hand & he pulls away. My cheeks turn red, but I try not to bring attention to it. Is this man really avoiding me? Was he just playing nice to get into my panties? Nonna Razza warned me about guys like this. They will tell you anything you want to hear just to get your Fiore which is flower in Italian. Or as Grandma Harper used to say my "goodies". I still to this day find it awkward talking about my vagina when I think of how Nonna & Grandma used to talk.

I look over at Maya who is giving me a raised brow. I think I better take her aside & tell her what's going on with Henry & Derrick.

"Ladie's room Maya?" I ask.

"Thought you'd never ask, this is my 3rd mimosa & I better hurry off before my 4th gets back." She says jokingly.

<h1 style="text-align:center">Chapter 22</h1>

I walk into the bathroom behind Mya & shut the door & lock it so nobody else can walk in behind us.

"My God Lana, what is up with you this morning. Paranoid much?" Mya says in a sarcastic tone as she flips her hair in the mirror. "I wasn't even this paranoid the time I slept with that guy who turned out to be married the next morning when his wife showed up at home while I was in their bathtub." she says with her hand on her hip now looking at me in the mirror.

"Ok so you know I slept with Henry last night, but what you don't know is right before THAT happened Derek sent me a gushy text about still loving me!" I blurt out. "And now," I sigh "Henry is acting off….. like as if it was just a one night stand or something but he didn't give off that vibe before. Do you think I made a mistake?" I ask looking at my best friend desperate for her brutal, honest, truth I need right now.

But Mya surprises me & does the exact opposite. She looks at me in the mirror still dropping her hand from her hip & turning on the faucet. She starts hysterically laughing & flinging cold water at me. "Hot stuff, look at you all the boys want your goodies." She says laughing so loud I shush her in case anyone is listening.

"Mya, be serious I need you to be honest with me like you always are. What should I do?" I ask frantically.

She turns off the faucet, turns around and grabs me by the shoulders & begins to shake me. "Lana, relax dude. You slept with Henry big deal & honestly good for you it is about time you got some good man candy in your bed. You have been so uptight forever. Who cares even if it was a one-night stand. Stop thinking so hard about this, we are at the beach. We are having fun. And we are together. Don't you remember what fun is like? Just enjoy the ride Lana. Let it happen at its own pace. And definitely do NOT ask him if it was a one-night stand. And please for the love of God do not ask him if you were good. Act confidently & hold your head up high. Act like you belong with me, geesh." She says and then she rolls her eyes.

"And what about Derek?" I ask her as she lets go of me & turns around to now use the ladies room.

"Dude, he's gonna be in love with you for life. Look at you, you're the literal best he will ever have. He is probably realizing what a mistake he made & I am thinking it has to do with that picture I posted last night." Mya says.

I turn my head to look at her even though she is currently sitting on the toilet. "Mya Penelope…. What picture?" I ask with a heavy sigh.

"Oh, nothing crazy just you yesterday in your hot as shit pink bathing suit by the pool before we went out on the town." She smiles.

"YOU DIDN'T!" I gasp.

"I did & by the way you're welcome that picture has well over 200 likes on it & I only posted it last night." She says smiling & straightening herself up as she stands.

"Oh my …. MYA!" I shout as I open my phone app to facebook & see she is right she posted me in my bathing suit. I am looking up at the sky with my white sunglasses & I look….. happy & GOOD? I actually look good. For once I don't point out the gray hairs at the top of my head or the thickness to my hips & thighs. You can't even see the cellulite I have on my inner thighs; I look REALLY GOOD.

"Mya" I say in a frustrated tone…… she looks at me about to defend herself…. But I grab her & pull her into a tight embrace. "I love you Mya. Thank you." I say as I hug her tighter. "You always know how to make me feel….good." I breathe out as I relax into our hug.

"What are friends for you spoiled brat." She says as we both laugh.

I look at her & tears fill my eyes. "I guess I needed this more than I knew. You really are the best friend Mya." I say as I wipe my tears from my eyes.

"I know I am" she laughs as she herself wipes a tear away. "Now let's get back to our men before some other hussies try to snatch them up." She says & unlocks the door.

I smile & realize why we are best friends.

Friendship really is the love you sometimes need.

Chapter 23

After Henry & JC left us Mya & I decide to head upstairs to rest after our long, adventurous evening.

"I hope you didn't get down & dirty in my bed last night." Mya snorts before jumping on her bed.

"Mya shut up, really." I say. "Hey, do you think everything was ok with Henry the way we left it at the pool?" I ask Mya.

"Lana, you have to chill the fuck out girl. Nobody wants a stage 5 clinger. Don't you know men love what they can't have. Make yourself a little more unavailable sometimes." She says.

I look at her in shock because is she really saying this to me? Ms. I sleep with you on the first date. "And what about you miss. I am ready to bang your brains out the night I meet you." I say. Mya scoots to the edge of her bed & smiles. "I didn't say don't give it up I just said don't be so clingy. Henry obviously likes what you've got to give so you gave him a taste now wait it out. He will be running back. He is probably just scared because you're an animal in the sac." Mya says with a big smile on her face before she rolls onto her back & kicks her sandals off. "Now get some sleep bitch because tonight is a best friend's night." She says before she rolls onto her side & falls asleep.

I look over at my beautiful best friend & think about all the adventures we've had in the past & I wonder what we could possibly do to top some of our past wild years. I check my phone one more time before I cozy under my blankets & fall asleep. Nothing but a text from the kids saying they love me. Nothing from Henry & nothing more from Derrick.

"Where have you been Derek it's 1 am. I know your meeting didn't go past 9pm so what the hell is going on?" I shout in a quiet tone since the kids are sound asleep just in the other room. "Why are you always assuming the worst Ed took us all for drinks after the meeting. What's the big deal? It's not like we had plans or anything. All you care about is the kids or the house or your grandmother. You never even ask me what I'm doing anyways so why start now?" Derek shouts back in a loud tone. I hear the baby monitor go off & realize Carson is waking up for his next feeding. "Great, now you woke up Carson. You can't expect me to put my motherly duties aside so we can go out for drinks with your boss Derek. I have responsibilities & both of them are sleeping next door & are also YOUR responsibility too! Or did you forget that?" I am now speaking louder then before. "Whatever Lana, I am tired. Go feed the baby & forget it." Derek says. I walk past him closing my bathrobe & look back before I leave the room. "I love you Derek. I really do." I say so soft he doesn't even hear me.

Chapter 24

I wake from my dream to the sound of Mya snoring & notice the sun has nearly set. I look over at my phone to a missed call from Derek & a new text from Henry. Wow & when I fell asleep I had nothing. I look at the time & my phone says 6:45 pm. Holy crap we slept almost 5 hours straight. I quietly slip out of bed to pee. I open the text from Henry & it just says "hi." Well this can't be good. I think to myself. I look at my missed call & notice Derrick left a voicemail. I listen & it says "Hey L, listen about last night I had a few brewskis I was tanked. Don't even sweat it. Love ya." WHAT A DICK. I say out loud. Mya is suddenly knocking on the bathroom door. "Did you lock the door seriously Lana who the fuck did you think was going to come in and watch you pee?" She shouts from outside. I jump up & open it then wash my hands. "Wow crazy much?" I say. "What the fuck crawled up your ass while you were sleeping? Or should I say who?" she snorts with laughter. "Sorry I just, I got a tex….. let's get ready & go find an adventure." I say with a smile on my face. "Oh me likey, what kind of adventure is Lana Piranha thinking?" She asks excitedly. I flip my hair & smile "Something wild that we will remember forever." I say.

After we get all dolled up in the sexiest outfits we have well the sexiest outfits Mya has. Again I am wearing her clothes & I am seriously regretting it this time. I am in a pair of black high waisted short shorts with a gold halter top that shows a little of my midriff. A crop top if you will. And Mya has on a sexy red dress that honestly looks like it could be an apron I wear in the kitchen. It is missing so much material that if she turns the right way you may get a glimpse of her full breasts. But Mya of course pulls it off very well with her amazing figure. I on the other hand feel a little uncomfortable since the shorts are so short my thighs rub together while I am walking &

I won't lie it's pretty uncomfortable. "So what kind of adventure are we going on?" "Should we hit the lounge?" she says. I look around & think. I see the lobby & there is a huge sign by the door that says "Donahue Wedding Ballroom 100". I look over at Mya & point." Let's go there." I say as I burst out laughing. Mya looks up, reads the sign & says "Alright let's go."

"Mya, I was kidding. We can't just waltz into someone's WEDDING. We aren't even invited guests." I whisper shout at her. She turns her head & laughs. Then she bolts towards the ballroom & function rooms. I chase her down the hall as she stops in front of a giant set of doors with beautiful white flowers all on the outer frame of the door. She glances back at me with an evil smile before she pushes the doors open.

"Mya, stop!" I shout but it is to late we are in the middle of the Donahue wedding. "Shit." I whisper. Everyone is walking around & talking so they don't even notice us. It looks like they are waiting for the bride & groom to arrive. I drag Mya out of the room & say "What the actual fuck is wrong with you we can't stay here Mya." I shout at her.

She keeps smiling & looks around before replying "Lana, are you going to have an adventure or are we going to go back upstairs & go to bed like elderly women." She asks. I sigh & turn my head just as a gorgeous woman in a beautiful white ballgown with intricate sequin patterns on the corset walks toward us. "Great dress!" Mya says. "Thank you." The bride says in a soft tone. Mya nods & asks the bride if she is ready & the bride nods as a man in an all-black tux walks up behind her & grabs her hand. The bride shakes her head yes & Mya says "okay, & who are we announcing again?" with a huge smile on her face. "Kathrine & Ryan Donahue" she says.

Mya begins to open the door & says "Excellent." She motions me to hold the door while she draws the full attention in the room to us

"For the first time everyone stand & welcome Mr. & Mrs. Katherine & Ryan Donahue." The room stands & cheers as Mya waves them on & smiles. She is truly good at this. A little too good at this. At my wedding she got drunk & sat in the corner making mean faces at Derek. But then again, she was never his biggest fan.

I follow behind closing the doors & adjusting the florals as I walk in. I try to make very little eye contact with everyone. But luckily as expected the bride is of course stealing the show so nobody notices the two unbelonging wedding guests here.

"Mya, pssst Mya." I whisper softly. She turns with a big smile on her face to me.

"You think it's open bar? Or do they strike you as the kind of couple who says; nah, let them pay for their own beer & wine?" Mya says to me as she turns on her heel to head for the bar.

I grab her arm & whisper in her ear "don't you think they will notice two strangers at the bar?"

"I think they will notice two strangers grabbing each other at the front door." She says to me sarcastically.

I release her as she skips happily over to the bar. "Howdy, I will do your signature drink this evening please. Two of them." She says sweetly to the female bartender.

"No problem. That will be $18.85 would you like to open a tab?" says the bartender.

"Nah, just the two drinks will do." Mya says.

"I told you we will be noticed!" I say as a gentleman approaches us at the bar.

"Ladies, how are we doing this evening? May I buy you beautiful girls a drink?" says the gentleman standing before us in a stunning all black suit with a pink tie. He is older but very attractive.

"Sure can!" says Mya as she winks at him. "I'm Maura & this is Lucy." She says.

I gasp not knowing what to say but when the gentleman goes to shake my hand I place my hand in his and allow him to greet me. "Ni—Nice to meet you sir." I say.

"The pleasure is mine. I am George Hawthorne. Father of the bride. I take it you must be on Ryan's side." He says smiling.

Before I can even open my mouth Mya interjects. "Ryan is a good friend of mine we go way back. We went to college together. Katherine is a beautiful bride. What a lucky man Ryan is." She says charmingly. Like I said she is too good at this.

"Splendid!" George says. "Anything these beautiful ladies want this evening will go on my tab please Beth." He says to the female bartender. "No problem Mr. Hawthorne." The woman says.

"Mya, I don't think this is such a good idea." I whisper to her as she hands me my drink which looks like a pina colada but a less sugary version.

"Relax LUCY, & have a little fun for ONCE." She says in a vexed tone as she rolls her eyes.

"Okay, it's your funeral at a wedding." I say laughing as I take a sip of my drink. Turns out it's delicious too.

"May I expect a dance from one of you ladies or maybe both before the evening is up?" George says to us.

"Oh you can count on it." Mya tells George in a flirtatious voice.

"Why not." I say.

The dance floor begins to fill up when I see George's eyes meet mine. He begins to stride towards me. Before I can do anything Mya pushes her drink towards me & says "I will take the first spin around the floor for us. You got get us two more of whatever the fuck these fruity drinks are."

She meets George halfway & they begin to spin around towards the dance floor. I take it Mr. Hawthorne does not have a Mrs. Hawthorne as his date or else she may not be too pleased with the likes of what's happening.

I take in a deep breath as I turn away from the sight of Mya dirty dancing with the bride's father as everyone claps & cheers them on. God she is confident.

"Hi there, can we please get two more of these?" I ask the woman behind the bar. Beth, I think her name is.

"Sure, thing sweetheart." She says.

I look back & the song is ending Mya walks towards me with George.

"You're up pretty lady." He says to me putting his hand out for me to grab.

I begin to thank God they are now playing a smooth slow song.

I spin around the dance floor with George when I notice the bride talking to her guests pointing at us. I look over at Mya who is downing both her drink & mine now flirting with the male bartender.

"You look lovely tonight." George whispers in my ear.

"Why thank you I feel very underdressed." I say. Knowing I am not dressed for a formal wedding, but I am still dressed somewhat dolled up.

"So, I notice you have no wedding ring on. Am I to assume you are available?" he asks.

"Oh, I am divorced." I respond.

"Wow, someone was foolish enough to let you go. What a shame for them, but what a delight for me." He says as his hands trail down to my bottom.

I look over at Mya who is ignoring the groping situation going on right now. Then I glance back to the bride who is now striding towards us.

"Really Daddy, must you be this way at my wedding! Mom is right over there you know!" she says as she gives me a dirty look.

"I am so sorry." I say.

She still looks at me with disgust.

Mya glances over her shoulder & waves me over.

"Thank you for the dance, Mr. Hawthorne." I say.

"Anytime pretty lady." He says with a wink.

I rush off the floor towards Mya. "We better get out of here." I turn back & see Mr. Hawthorne & his daughter arguing on the dancefloor. Just when her husband walks over & they all glance up at us.

"We better go, NOW!" I say.

"The husband begins to walk towards us with his head tilted."

"Mya, we have a problem." I say as Mya continues to flirt with the bartender.

"Ladies, I'm sorry I can't remember how we know each other." He says with a smile.

Mya flips her hair & spins around leaning up against the bar while facing the groom. "Ryan Donahue…. You disappointed me. You don't remember your old college roommate's girlfriend?" she says.

"You dated Smitty?" he says.

"Did I date Smitty? I broke his heart." Mya says with a wink.

"No shit. You're the one he was crying over junior year for a week?" he says.

"I sure am. & I hold that scoundrel deep in my heart for what I did to him. But two ships in the night as they say." She says with a big smile.

"And I'm sorry you are?" he says looking at me.

I lift my hand to shake his but before I can say anything Mya interjects. "This is my new fling." She says.

"Oh, well pleased to meet you…?" he says

"Lucy…." I say

"Lucy, nice to meet you." He says shaking my hand.

"I do not remember inviting anyone from school. How did you ladies hear about this." He asks.

"Ironically Ryan, our good friend Billy Flannigan was invited but couldn't make it so I figured why not take his place."

"Oh my God you know Billy too! What a small world!" he shouts.

"Billy, Billy, Billy …. He's a good friend of mine." Mya says.

"Well enjoy the night & thanks for coming." He says.

I grab Mya as he turns away. " Okay who the hell are these people & what are you even talking about?" I ask frantically.

She watches while he walks back to his bride & waits until they kiss & seem to calm down.

"Shut up Lana, relax." She says as she turns back around. "Bill Flannigan has a place tag at the front of the room that sits at an empty seat." I used the first name I saw of an empty seat. I took a guess & looks like it worked." She says.

Before I can even respond she asks the bartender for his number & the bride is suddenly heading our way.

"Hi ladies, I am not sure we have formally met. I seem to have thought you ladies worked here. Not guests of mine." She says in a not so sweet voice.

"Maura Paul." Nice to meet you says Mya. "And this is my girlfriend, Lucy Rodriguez." She adds.

"Nice to meet you ladies, & I am told you know my husband? Ryan?" she asks with a questioning tone.

"Since sophomore year of college." Mya says.

"Oh so you went to…… what was the name of you guys' school again?" asks the bride.

"You don't know Ryan's glory days at school? He never told you where went & what a popular guy he was?" Mya asks.

"I know what school my husband went to, but I am not sure you do. Before I have you thrown out for trespassing, I would really like you to leave." She says.

"Oh sweetie, I am sorry we ruffled your feathers dancing with your dad & joking with your husband, but I assure you we are not toying with you." Mya says.

I put my face in my hand knowing this is going to end badly. "I like your dress. Remember I told you that when you walked into the hallway?" I say.

They both shoot a look at me & I have never wanted to disappear so badly.

"So you think because you told me you liked my dress you can come to my wedding?" she asks.

"I mean, it is a great dress." Mya says. Sipping her drink.

"Yeah, well we are going to just keep this a closed event. Please leave." She says.

"Katherine, come on girl. I do really love that dress." Mya says.

"Again, we are going to keep this closed." She says as she motions towards the door.

"I'm so sorry, we will head out." I say.

"I'm not as sorry as her." Mya says gulping down her drink & following me out.

I am mortified as we walk out & Mr. Hawthorne motions for me to "call him".

Chapter 25

"That was horrible!" I say to Mya. As she laughs & laughs & laughs in the hallway.

"Oh my God relax Lana." she says. "On the plus side, if Henry doesn't pan out I think that dad really liked you." She begins to laugh even louder slapping me on the ass.

"Funny." I say rolling my eyes.

"What, like you couldn't use a sugar daddy? Or just some good old sugar?" she manages to get out through giggles.

"Now can we please just go to the lounge?" I say

"Hold up, look down there." She says as she points down another hallway towards the largest ballroom the hotel offers.

"The Grand Master Ballroom. What about it?" I ask.

"Looks like another wedding. Let's go." She says pulling my wrist.

"Mya, are you crazy we just got kicked out of the last one!" I whisper shout.

"Live a little. Sheesh. Wasn't that the most thrilling thing we've done this week?" Mya says staring at me with pleading eyes.

"One more wedding Mya & if we get kicked out of this one I am going upstairs & packing my things." I say in a sassy tone.

"Deal." She says.

However, we both know I won't be going anywhere since Mya drove us here.

This wedding is loud. The closer we get to the room the more I can feel the vibrations from the music & laughter coming from inside. I can already tell this is a completely different type of crowd in here.

We walk in & I am shocked at what I see.

Chapter 26

The Grand Master Ballroom looks just like the front lobby. There is a giant water fountain in the middle of the room with gorgeous crystal lights & chandeliers surrounding us. The room is full of guests & this wedding looks a little more casual. I can tell by the guests attire.

"Oh my God look at that bar!" My exclaims.

I turn my head to the direction she is facing. Okay that does look pretty cool. The bar is on the patio in a big U shape facing the ocean. Wow this room really is exquisite. "Should we get a drink?" I ask.

"Duh, was waiting on you." Mya says.

We scurry over to the bar & we are laughing the whole way as we pass a ton of good-looking men.

"What will you ladies be having this evening?" the handsome bartender asks.

"What is the signature drink tonight?" Mya inquires.

"Open bar & every drink is the signature drink." Says the bartender as he shows us a big sign on the edge of the bar.

It reads "Drinks on us – get what y'all like & stay all night!"

"Well alright then two fruit seltzers" Mya says.

I smile re-reading the sign again. "Y'all". They must be southern I think to myself.

The bartender hands us our drinks & I reach in my bag to tip him & he stops me.

"No tips allowed from guests." He says with a wink & a gorgeous smile.

"No tips?" I question.

"The Bride & Groom requested we not accept tips from guests – only from them at the end of the evening." He says.

"Well, I insist I leave this tip here." I say as a slide a $10 bill over to him.

He laughs. "You are a rule breaker I see." He says with another gorgeous smile. His dimples are quite charming.

Mya bumps my arm with her elbow. "So, what's your name Mr. Cocktail?" she asks while she sips her fruity hard seltzer.

"Von" he says.

"Nice to meet you Von. I am Lana & this is Mya." I say with a smile.

"Nice to meet you ladies too. Come back & see me again. Will ya?" he asks with a wink as he turns to tend to the customers at the other end of the bar.

"Okay girlfriend, looks like you got yourself another admirer tonight." Mya says. "I am just wondering who you will pick to take home with you when the trip is over. Henry, George, or Von?" she bursts out laughing.

"Mya, knock it off." I say.

We continue to walk around & notice trays of appetizers & hot food everywhere all around. There is a giant heart shaped table with deserts which is exactly where I head. Mya has stopped at the hot food section & is piling filet mignon & prime rib with gravy onto her plate. While I take a plate & fill it with donuts, cakes, & of course scones. My favorite.

We walk around an empty table on the outdoor patio connected to the ballroom & sit down together.

"How is the food?" I ask Mya as she cuts into her second piece of prime rib.

"Oh it tastes RICH. Figuratively & literally." She says.

I smile at her. I love how Mya just owns who she is. I wish I could be more confident in my own identity just as she is.

"In case you were wondering the dessert table is fully stocked." I say as I bite into my mini éclair.

"Yes, I see that as is your plate." She says with a mouthful of prime rib.

We both giggle & keep eating. We are so consumed by our food & drink we barley notice the bride sitting alone at the table next to us drinking champagne & looking out at the water. While all her guests enjoy her special day.

"Mya, look, the bride is alone right next to us." I say.

Mya looks up & before I know it she is waving her over to sit with us.

The bride stands & strides over with a very forced smile on her face.

"How y'all doing tonight?" she asks.

"We are great thanks & you look stunning!" I say. I notice now that she is standing she isn't wearing a real wedding gown. Her top is a white satin camisole with sparkling applique all along the bottom hem. But on the bottom half she wears a very short & tight jean skirt with the most beautiful cowgirl boots I have ever seen. They are white & shiny like they just came out of the box. They have this beautiful design all down the sides & they are covered from top to bottom in diamonds. I am awe struck by these boots.

"The boots huh?" she asks while I drool over them.

"Wow, those are badass." Mya says.

"I am in love with them!" I say as my eyes shoot back up to her from the boots.

"A little pre wedding gift from my husband. I wanted them so bad & he got them to surprise me with. I was going to wear my old basic cowgirl boots but these feel much more fitting." She says.

"Well, they are hot." Mya says.

She sits down with us & takes a sip from her glass. "So, you ladies having fun?" she asks.

I smile nervously & look down at my disgusting plate full of probably 500 grams of sugar on it. "It is a beautiful evening. Are you having a good time?" I ask.

"Of course she is, she is a hot ass bride & there's amazing food here." Mya says.

The bride laughs. "I'm Tiffany." She replies.

"We know that." Mya says.

"Do you now?" Tiffany says.

"Yeah, we are friends of the grooms side." Mya winks.

I look down at my drink anxiously before I pick it up & take a sip.

"Oh yeah – Todd's side?" asks Tiffany.

"Exactly, Todd's side." Mya says.

I look back & fourth between the two of them.

"That's funny." Says Tiffany.

"Why?" asks Mya.

"Because my husband's name is Conner." She says with a big smile & gulps down her drink.

"Fuck." Mya says out loud.

"I am so sorry. We will head out now." I say as I go to stand.

"Sit down ladies. Nobody has to leave." She says as she smiles bigger.

"I am just happy to see a couple of faces who don't want to take a photo with me or talk my ear off about my dad." She says.

"Why is that stuff bad?" Mya asks

"If you're Frankie Divine's daughter it is." She says.

"Frankie Divine!?" I shout.

"Shhhh, keep it down I didn't want anyone to notice me out here."
She says in a whisper.

"Sorry but did you say THE Frankie Divine?' I ask again.

She nods & grabs a scone from my plate & takes a bite.

"Yupp I am formerly Tiffany Divine. But now I am thrilled to no
longer be connected to that name. I am Tiffany McMills." She says
brightly.

"I'm lost who the fuck is Frankie Divine?" Mya asks.

"Only the most talked about "mobster" in New York." I say with
air quotes to Mya.

"Oh shit." I knew I liked you she says winking at Tiffany taking
another bite of her food dipping it in the gravy first.

"Yeah well daddy wanted the best of the best for his little girl.
Even though we barely speak. I moved to Texas about 5 years ago
when I finished at NYU. That is how I met Conner." Says Tiffany.

"Wow, I have seen you before on the news but only a glimpse of
you." I say to her realizing I may be out of line so I apologize
quickly.

"Don't be sorry --- you think you're the first one to say something
to me. Please honey half the people here I do not even know."

I smile at her with a look of sympathy.

"My husband Conner comes from a very small family. Nothing
like mine. My family guest list was over 100 people alone. His was
24. Our friends combined that was a little longer. But my dad's
guests that was where the extra 175 people came in." she says.

"That must be tough." I say.

"Not so bad I get a lot of good with the bad. But I just wanted a simple wedding. Something in Texas out in the ranch me & Connor bought together. I hate the hustle & bustle of the city. So when daddy said he wanted it up here I chose to do the reception here. It isn't as bad as a busy city in NY." She says.

"Well you certainly know how to throw a party." Mya says as she cheers' the bride.

She laughs. "Y'all are funny." She says. "So what do I call you girls?" she asks us.

"I am Lana & this is my best friend Mya." I say.

"Well Howdy Lana & Mya. Stay as long as you want & enjoy everything. I love having you & from now on you better say you're a guest of mine because Connor has a list so small we can all memorize the guests names from his list." She laughs & stands to leave waving as she goes.

"What luck!" Mya says with that devious smile on.

And I know we are in for a long night of trouble now.

Chapter 27

Henry;

I wonder if I should text her. No, I don't want her to think I am a stalker. But what if she thinks I am blowing her off after last night. No, I don't want her to get the wrong idea, but I also don't want to force her into anything she isn't ready for. I saw the text from her ex-husband last night after she went to sleep. I wasn't snooping I just wanted to plug her phone in for her & it lit up on the screen when I plugged it in. I am sure she would rather get back with her husband than start all over with a teacher/ farmer/widower of two kids. Besides she didn't even want to make plans for tonight. JC said he got a text from Mya saying it was a girl's night they will see us one more time before they leave. Maybe I should have never made myself so available to a woman who is so independent & strong. What use does she have for a guy like me. I put my phone down & lay back on the bed looking at the ceiling. "Don't blow this Henry." I say to myself.

Chapter 28

The music is so loud in this room I can barely hear myself think. I watch as Mya twirls & turns in the arms of some guy with a cowboy hat on. She looks so beautiful & carefree.

I walk out onto the outdoor patio. The wind feels amazing against my warm skin damp with sweat from being in the middle of the dance floor.

"Much nicer out here. Isn't it?" – a voice asks me.

I turn to see who it is, but their back is to me.

"Yes, the breeze is lovely & I must admit the noise level was beginning to get to me." I say.

The broad shoulders in a dark suit jacket lifts a glass to his mouth before turning back to look at me over his shoulder.

"Phillip Divine." He says.

"You are Tiffany's older brother." I say.

"Guilty." He says.

"How do you fit in here?" he asks me.

"I am a last minute added guest." I shrug & say shyly.

"You a cop?" he asks.

I laugh so loud I think I snort embarrassingly. "A cop? Me?" I laugh out.

"Why is that so funny? Wouldn't be the first time we had some cops invite themselves to our family events." He says.

"I assure you, I am no cop. Although my teenage daughter believes I worked for the FBI with how well I can always figure out when she is lying to me." I say.

"Well, moms are sometimes more dangerous than a federal agent anyways." He says. Then he raises his glass to me. "To moms." He says & throws the rest of his drink back.

"To moms." I say.

"So do you have a name? FBI?" he asks.

"Lana." I say.

"Beautiful name fitting for a beautiful woman." He says.

"Well, someone's more charming than the newspaper lets off." I say.

"Well, only someone who still reads the newspapers might find that charming." He says.

I blush. As he gets closer to me his facial features in the light are kind of intimidating because they are near perfect. I look away so he doesn't notice my staring.

"Lana, can I get you a drink? I need to go refill my scotch." He says.

"Oh sure, a glass of chardonnay?" I reply.

"Chardonnay it is." He tells me as he walks past me to the bar.

His suit is expensive & the scent of sandalwood & leather lingers in the air as he passes me. Lana, stop being so promiscuous. I think to myself. Geesh one week with Mya & my morals are right out the window. I have so far had a one-night stand, flirted with someone's dad, and now someone's brother. Get it together you're bordering floosy territory.

Phillip comes back & hands me a wine glass half full of a sweet smelling aroma.

"California Ripe Chardonnay for the lady." He says.

"Thank you." I say almost in a whisper.

He sits beside me on the bench I am sitting on looking out towards the ocean. The lights behind us are dim but still allow me to get a very good look at the man next to me. His eyes are dark unlike his sisters. Tiffany has light eyes almost hazel I would say. But his are so dark they could be black. His facial features are simply exquisite. A strong chin & beautiful cheekbone. He looks like a Greek God of mythology.

"You are very beautiful." He says to me. "I am almost intimidated sitting next to such a beauty."

"What!" I snort out. Almost spitting my wine, I just sipped. "You think I am intimidating? Please you are Phillip freakin' Divine!" I nearly shout as I burst into an unflattering laugh.

"Yes, and you are Lana freakin……..?" he says questioningly.

"Pais… Harper." I say. "Harper is my maiden name."

"Ahhh, divorced?" he asks. "Sounds like a fool if he walked away from you." Phillip says.

"Phillip Divine is also divorced." I reply.

"Call me Phil, & yes, I have divorced twice as a matter of fact. Seems I cannot find the right woman for me." He says.

Damn. He is fine. I look over my shoulder to check on Mya & it seems she is still dancing away the night with her cowboy.

"So, why are you out here all alone?" I ask.

He sips his scotch & looks at me with an eyebrow raised.

"I thought we had this discussion, its nicer out here." He says.

"Yeah, not buying it. It is pretty nice but what are you doing all alone outside of your own sister's wedding?" I ask.

"Weddings are not my favorite. Only a true divorcee might understand my feelings." He says as he raises his glass before sipping his scotch again.

I swallow slowly. Thinking of his words he just spoke. He is not wrong. I am not a big fan of weddings ever since my divorce I don't hate them but if I could avoid them. I would. Then again it is much easier attending weddings of total strangers than attending those of people I know.

"I can understand that." I say.

"Are you here with someone?" he asks.

"Yes, I am. My best friend Mya." I say.

"So, no date?" he asks.

"Mya is my date." I say sipping my drink with a big smile on my face.

"Well maybe you wouldn't mind accompanying me back in there as my date?" he says.

I loudly swallow this time. I look over to him with probing eyes. "Why would you want me to be your date?" I asked shocked.

"A beautiful girl who is here dateless. Why not?" he asks.

"You could probably find a better-looking date then me." I scoff.

"Doubt it. They eye of the beholder is never wrong." He tells me.

"I...I guess I could sit with you inside for a while." I say nervously.

He stands & puts his arm out for me to take. "Shall we?" he asks.

I stand & lock my arm through his. "Ok." I say.

Chapter 29

Mya;

I look all around & can't find that sly little fox anywhere. She better not have left me. I will kick her ass for being such a scaredy cat. Even after we were literally welcomed by the bride. Where the heck could she have gone.

Chapter 30

We walk in our arms locked together. I am wondering why he would want to have me on his arm of all women. I'm not sure why but all I am thinking is that Mya might look better with this man than me. I point her out to him as we walk by. He nods & keeps walking.

"Everyone, this is Lana." He introduces me to the people at his table.

They all smile & say hello.

I smile & say hello as well.

Phillip pulls out my chair & I sit with him drinking my chardonnay down to the last drop.

He leans into my side "Another glass?" he softly whispers into my ear.

The hairs on my neck standing & chills run through my body. This man is dangerously sexy.

"Please." I say handing him my glass.

"Coming right up beauty." He says with a wink.

As he rounds the room to the bar I am sitting alone with the table.

"So Lana, how do you know Phillip?" a handsome younger man asks me. He is sitting next to a stunning blonde with large breasts. She is wearing a blue sequin dress that is so short & tight she looks as though she may bust out of it at any second.

"We just met recently." I say.

"And here you are at our table." Says the woman.

"So, it seems." I say.

I have never felt more out of place in my life.

Phillip comes back & hands my drink to me. He sists down & pulls me to his side.

"So Chuck, how's business?" he asks the older gentleman at our table.

"Slow Phil, slow as usual." He says raising his eyebrow.

"Gloria how are the kids?" he asks the woman with the older gentleman called Chuck.

"They are growing well." She says sipping her red wine.

"And you Phillip? How are you doing?" the busty blonde asks him.

"I am fan-fucking-tastic P." he says to the woman.

"Grow up Phillip will you?" she says.

"Why Penny…. Is it a coincidence you're here with my cousin?" he asks.

I suddenly know what's going on. Penny is his ex-wife. She was a swimsuit model. I can't remember where I saw her but now it makes sense. She & Phillip had a huge wedding just like this & divorced only a month after.

"I was invited you bastard." she says to him crossing her arms over her chest.

"Hey, man I didn't think you'd care. I told you I was seeing her." The younger gentleman says.

"Nah I don't care man. But you should know a whore when you see one. You know better than that Mikey." He says to the younger gentleman now known as Mikey.

Wow. You can't get this from a newspaper or magazine. I am right in the middle of a TMZ story.

I lean into Phillp's side & whisper. "Should I go?" I ask him.

He looks down at me as if to respond but instead he kisses me! He plants a giant kiss on me. And I'd be lying if I didn't say the kiss was really fucking good. But I pull back surprised & don't take my eyes off him, nor does he take his off me.

I am breathing shallow when I spot Mya staring at me with a huge grin on her face from the bar.

She grabs her drink & walks towards us but I shake my head not to. She stops in her tracks & waves me over.

I look at Phillip & motion to her & he nods at me to go to her.

I walk up to Mya & she grabs my hand & screams.

"So are you going to tell me about the hot as fuck mafia looking guy you were just viciously making out with in front of the entire wedding?" she asks.

"That's Phillip Divine." I say to her, still catching my breathe from what just happened.

"The dad!!?!?!?!" she asks.

"No Mya that's Frankie Divine. Remember?" I ask her.

"I don't know Lana. So, who the fuck is that one?" she asks.

"The older brother." I say.

"Get it girl." She says back.

I laugh at her. "He just randomly kissed me, & he asked me to be his date for the rest of the wedding." I say seeking her approval.

"YES, YES, YES!" she shouts squeezing my hand.

"You see that cowboy & the nerdy looking guy?" she asks me.

"Yes." I reply.

"Well I am spending my night with them – they asked me to sit with them. Well technically it was supposed to be us but you have your hands full now." She says.

"Mya!" I exclaim.

"Go, do your thing & we will catch up in a while." She says.

"Okay but no leaving without the other one Mya Penelope."

"Deal" she says rolling her eyes.

The night goes on & as I spend more time with Phillip, I realize he is nothing like I have read about. He is kind of gentle & sweet. I am sure he is a shark when he needs to be but with me he is showing his most vulnerable attributes.

"Would you like to dance?" he asks me.

"Why, I would love to." I reply.

I notice his ex, Penny is watching us like a hawk. As beautiful as she is on the outside so far she has proven to be very ugly on the inside. I wonder why his family would sit her at his table.

As we spin around the dance floor to some dirty rap song, I notice Tiffany & her husband sharing their cake together at the head table. They look so happy. For a moment you might believe in fairy tales. But that gets you nowhere. Fairy Tales don't exist & the boy next door turns out to be a cheating bastard who ruins your life & leaves you with two kids to raise & a lifetime of insecurities.

"Hey, you, okay?" asks Phillip.

"Oh, yeah. Maybe I just drank a little to much wine." I reply as my cheeks redden.

"I can take you outside for some air. Come on." He says.

He takes my hand & pulls me back to the patio where we met. The night sky has gotten even darker. Very few stars line the sky tonight. The moon has risen so high that's about the only light you see.

"You can go back inside. No need to miss out on the fun being stuck out here with me." I say to him.

"What fun would it be if my date is out here?" he asks wrinkling his forehead & raising a brow.

"I'm sorry." I say.

"You know I have only known you about a few hours now but I have got to say you say sorry a lot." He says to me.

My face turns pink & I look away from him. "I'm sorry I know. I have been trying to work on it." I say realizing I have just said I'm sorry again.

Phillip smiles at me & brushes the hair from my face. He looks at me & leans in to kiss me again. I pull back this time.

"Look, I am sorry if I gave you the wrong impression, but I am newly divorced, I think I am kind of seeing someone I met here but I am really not sure how these things work anymore, oh & I have two kids." I blurt out realizing only afterwards how pathetic I must sound.

Phillip pulls back & his smile fades.

Great, he is thinking the same thing as I am. Pathetic.

"Do you know why I asked you to be my date tonight?" says Phillip.

"Because you wanted to make your ex jealous." I say.

"Well, that & I find you very beautiful. I can feel your pain though. I can feel it because I, to have the same pain." He says.

"My pain?" I ask very confused.

"A beautiful woman like you standing alone outside of a big party looking out into the water struggling to regulate her breathing & calm her wandering mind is feeling something painful." He says.

"I guess, but you could tell all that by looking at me once?" I say.

"Your eyes, they speak a lot louder than you do." He utters.

"You know for someone who is portrayed as a ruthless savage you sure are poetic." I sigh as I speak. "My life is one complicated mess after the next. One minute I am standing in front of my bathroom mirror wondering when my life is going to feel…. Better….. or when I am going to feel… good again. Then I am here with my best friend who is wild & crazy but the most kind & generous woman you'd ever meet. And she's dragging me here pushing me to be the fun & vibrant girl I used to be. And when I do I meet a guy & I think wow he might be someone & what does he do? He sleeps with me & ignores me the next day like I was just some one-night stand. And from someone who married young I have never had a one-night stand. And now to top it all off the guy who I have seen all over the tabloids is kissing me at his sister's wedding." I sigh & look back at Phillip suddenly feeling even more embarrassed.

The silence is so loud I can feel my head spinning from the lack of words.

"I am so sorry I don't know why I just said all of that. I am sure the last thing a guy like you wants is someone like me spilling her suburban drama to you when you are just trying to……"

Phillip grabs my face & kisses me deeply. He holds my cheek in his left hand & the back of my head in his right hand. He works his tongue into my mouth & kisses me with such heat & fire I nearly stop breathing.

He pulls back & looks into my eyes "Don't ever apologize to me again for being yourself. I like that about you. You aren't like the girls I am used to being around. And as someone who is 41 years old I have been around a lot of girls." He says with a smirk.

I can barely catch my breath. My legs are shaking & my mind is blurry. I can't think straight. I need to find Mya & leave. This is to much.

"I'm sor- I hate to do this but I have to go." I say. "Thank you, Phillip, for being so kind to me tonight." I add before I stand & turn on my heels.

"Lana." He calls.

I look over my shoulder at him still trying to catch my breath.

Phillip walks up behind me & takes my hand spinning me around to face him. "Please, call me Phill. And I would really like to see you again. Even if it's for a cup of coffee or a walk around the neighborhood. Please can I see you again? Something about you gives me comfort." He says.

I sigh & wonder what the fuck this man sees in me that he wants to see ME again. I wonder if he has some mental issues.

"You want to see me again?" I say questioningly.

"Of course I do." He replies.

"Well, ok then." I say.

I motion for his phone & I put my number in it.

"I'll be calling you." He says.

I rush off before I regret what I have just done.

Chapter 31

I search for Mya & I see her by the exit.

"Hey!" I shout. "So much for not leaving the other behind." I say.

I can tell by looking at Mya she is pretty drunk at this point.

"Heyyyy Lana Piranah!!!! This is my best fucking friend guys." She shouts & grabs onto me.

Yupp, she is wasted.

"Mya, what have you done?" I ask.

"Oh please don't be mom Lana tonight be fun Lana." She says with a pouty face on.

"I am fun Lana. But how much did you drink?" I ask concerned.

"I am going to hang with my new friends Tommy & Sean." She says.

"Ok, where are we going?" I inquire.

"WE aren't going anywhere Lana, you go with your new friend & I will go with mine." She shouts.

"Mya, we stick together remember?" I say.

"Go have fun tonight Lana & so will I." she says.

I do not feel comfortable leaving her. I want to continue to protest but Mya is stubborn. She wants to do what she wants to do.

"I'm not that drunk Lana. I know what I am doing." She says noticing the look of concern on my face.

"I know, I just think we should stick together. I will be at our room. Will you meet me there?" I ask.

"You know it." She says & scurries off.

I grab the arm of the nerdy looking guy who I assume is named Sean.

"No funny business. Or I will find you." I say to him.

He gives me a nervous smile & says "nothing funny going on ma'am."

His southern accent tells me he is a friend of the groom.

"How do you know Conner the groom?" I ask.

"I am his younger brother. & Tommy is our cousin." He says.

I instantly feel more comfortable.

"We are going to the lounge in the lobby if you want to come with us." He says.

"It's okay, I know Mya wants to do her own thing. I will be in my room." I say.

"I'd love to accompany you to the lounge if you'd like to get out of here." Says a deep voice from behind me.

I turn & Phillip is there. This man is fine. But all I can think about is Henry for some reason. What would he think if I was in the lounge with another man. I wonder if he is in the lounge with JC. Why do I care? He hasn't even reached out to me & he was so distant at brunch.

"Well, I have to go to my room first. I need to get some more money." I say. Why the heck did I just agree to go with this guy.

"You don't need money. I have money." He says as he puts his arm out for me to take.

"Go on Sean. Catch up with your group. We will be behind you. & take good care of her friend." He says in an authoritative tone.

"No problem, Phill." He says.

I'm not sure what I am doing or getting myself into. But something about Phillip makes me feel wild. If it's possible I think he may be the darkness to the light Henry brought. Two guys in one week who find ME attractive. Two guys in one week who have given me attention. Wow. Maybe Mya was right.

Chapter 32

The lounge is packed. I think to myself, how many people can fit in this hotel. Because between the two weddings going on back there & all the guests at the hotel this place is like its own island.

"Would you like a drink?" Phillip asks me.

"Water." I say. "I am pretty sure I need a water break at this point."

"Water it is." He says as he makes his way to the bar top in the lounge.

I glance around but it's really hard to see anything. I don't see Mya anywhere in the mix of all these people. I turn around & see Phillip walking back to me with a bottle of water & a beer for himself.

"Water for the lady." He says as he hands me the bottle.

"Thanks. Do you want to head out to the beach?" I ask him.

"The club life is not your scene?" he asks.

"Not even a little bit." I shout.

We move out to the patio & I try to get a better view from outside. To see if I can see Mya. But it's like she knows I am looking for her & she is hiding very well in the crowd.

"I apologize if I overstepped by inviting myself. I just really didn't want the night to end." Says Phillip.

"I'm sorry you had to leave your sister's wedding. But thank you for reminding the guys to be gentleman. My friend Mya is kind of a free spirit, wildflower." I say.

"I did notice that about her." He says.

"She is one of a kind. She is my best friend. We have known each other almost as long as I have been alive." I say.

"It's nice to have friends like that." He says.

I sip my water & lean against the patio structure. I wonder if Henry is in there somewhere. I wonder if he will see me outside with another man. Will he be jealous?

"What's on your mind?" asks Phillip.

"Mya." I lie.

"Ah, wondering if she's still inside?" he asks.

"Why wouldn't she be?" I say.

"Well, she was having a good time with my sister's new in laws." He says.

I sigh because that's true. Mya is the type to follow her adventures solo.

"I know. I just like to keep a close eye on her. Whether she wants me to or not." I say.

"You're a good friend." He says.

I wonder how true that statement really is.

Chapter 33

Henry;

"I'm not in the mood for the lounge. It's almost midnight anyways." I say to JC.

"Dude, chill out the lounge is open until 3am. What's the problem?" he says.

"Just not feeling it. Don't you want to catch up with the girls?" I ask.

"The girls? Dude Mya made it clear they were going out on their own tonight. There is plenty more girls down at the lounge. Who cares. It's not like they're our girls anyways." Says JC.

He is used to having flings with girls. Not me. I don't just hook up like he does. I am a 35-year-old man. Not a 25-year-old boy.

"No they're not our girls YET." I say. "Besides didn't you say Mya was the best girl you've met in a long time?" I ask.

"Henry, she was awesome. But she isn't looking for anything. Trust me. I have met many girls like her. She isn't the settle down type. What's up with you tonight bro? You're off." Says JC.

"I just hit the drink to hard last night." I say.

"Well lighten up. The night is young." He says.

We get ready to head down to the lounge. I am not looking forward to watching JC hit on other girls tonight. All I can think about is what Lana is doing. And more importantly I want to know what she is thinking.

Chapter 34

Mya;

The lounge is packed full of people. I can't hear a fucking thing Tommy says to me. I like him, he's cute. But I also think Sean is cute too. Nerdy is not usually my type but what the hell. I'm on vacay. I am covered in sweat from the continuous dance moves I am currently busting out. Not to mention I am about 2 drinks away from being recognizably wasted.

"You want another drink sweet thang?" says Tommy.

"Yeah, I will take a fruit seltzer. Meet me outside I need some fresh air, I am hotter than Satan's mistress in here" I say.

I headed to the lounge patio. I stop at the door when I notice two familiar faces. This could be fun. I think.

"Well, well, well." I say to the two familiar faces.

"Mya, what are you doing here?" JC asks.

"Is Lana here?" Henry says looking hopeful.

"I am here with a couple friends. Lana went on her own adventure this evening." I say with a wink.

One thing about me is I don't like to give anyone the impression they have power over me. Especially a man. If they think they are your only option, you give them too much power. Lana is still learning now that she is single again. I have to teach her how it works.

"Oh, well ok then." JC says looking pitiful.

127

"See you boys around." I say & walk back inside.

Chapter 35

I am starting to feel exhausted. I finished my water & moved on to another drink. I am almost done with my drink when I see Mya sprint across the dancefloor to the bar.

"HEY! MYA!" I shout.

Mya continues to run past me. I don't doubt that she can't hear me, it is still so loud in here. Although the place has cleared out a bit it is still very hectic.

"MYA PENELOPE!" I shout even louder. Phillip nearly jumps out of his shoes next to me.

"That was for sure a mom voice." He says with a smile.

Mya turns her head & squints. She is trying to make out who called her as I quicken my steps towards her. Now that I am more visible to her sight, I see her eyes roll.

"Did you just call me by my full name, in that mom tone?" she says with another eye roll & her hands on her hips.

"I sure did." I say, proudly.

"What time are we staying here till?" I ask.

"Lana, I love you but go away. I don't need you to babysit me." She says to me.

"Mya, I get that, but you don't know these guys & we need to stick together. This is a girls night remember?" I ask.

"You're cramping my style kid." She says with a sassy look.

"I will lay low. Don't you worry." I laugh out.

Mya turns on her heels & waltzes over to the guys she is with. Grabbing her drink & flipping her hair she avoids me while enjoying her night.

"Is she always like this?" Phillip asks?

"Oh, absolutely. That's what I love about her." I say.

"Let's head out to the beach with our drinks." Mya shouts.

I follow behind grabbing hold of Phillips hand, so we don't get separated. Not sure why I do. But I kind of like having him around. He feels like a giant good-looking bodyguard.

We step onto the patio & I am jolted by the salty wind blowing in my face. There seems to be more of a chill in the air since last time we were outside.

"Need my jacket?" Phillip asks.

"Well then you will be cold." I say.

"Yes, but you will be warm. So that will warm me to warm you." He says sweetly.

"Poetic. Again." I say.

He drapes his suit jacket over my shoulders & I sip the fruity seltzer he got me from the bar.

I snuggle into the warmth of the large jacket. It smells like him. Sandalwood & leather.

"Lana, look who is here." I hear Mya shout from the table she & the guys are sitting at to my left.

I look around Phillip & see JC & Henry. Shit.

"How's it going. Phillip Divine." Says Phillip putting his hand in front of Henry to shake his.

I instantly turn red. And not like the normal embarrassed shade of red. I look like a tomato, or a fire engine. Thank God it is so dark out here.

"Henry Fields. & this is JC." Says Henry. Shaking Phillips' hand.

Fuck.

"So how do you two know each other?" Henry asks.

I look over at Mya who is laughing & smiling with her face in in Seans chest. Tommy next to them.

"We met at a wedding." I say.

"My sister got married tonight & Mya & Lana were there." says Phillip.

"Who the fuck cares." Says JC. Clearly, he cares.

Mya ignores him.

I look quickly between the guys. And realize I need to intervene.

"Henry, can we talk for a minute." I say.

"Ok, yeah." He says concerned.

We walk towards the edge of the water for a more private moment.

"I'm sorry." I say looking down.

"For what?" Henry says.

"I was waiting for you to call or text me." I say.

"So you thought hanging with some guy might make me jealous." He says.

"No, not at all. I just don't know how this works or how to do this." I say.

"It's pretty simple Lana. You like someone. You tell them. You sleep with them, you either date or move on. It's up to you how you want things to work out. Look, I'm not an idiot. I know you have got a lot going on. We just met. I know I am not your boyfriend." Henry says.

"I like you Henry. I wouldn't have done what I did if I didn't. I am not trying to make you jealous. He's just a really nice guy. I was hoping I would hear from you & when I didn't…." I pause & look down.

"You assumed this was a one-night type of thing?" Henry asks.

"Yeah…." I say.

I look to the ocean & back to Henry. "Not to mention you were so distant at brunch. Why?" I ask.

"I saw the text message from your ex. It freaked me out. I thought maybe this beautiful woman wants to be with her family." Henry says.

"WHAT?" I ask.

"Yeah. I was putting your phone on the…" Henry starts.

"You snooped through my phone? So much for we just met & it will go at my pace!" I shout without giving Henry a chance to continue.

"And another thing why the hell would you assume I wanted to go back to someone who literally cheated on me after I told you that in confidence?" I ask.

I start to storm off from Henry before I turn to him once more. "I really did like you Henry. And yes, I was hoping this would be more. But maybe I was the one being an idiot." I say before continuing my dramatic storm off.

"I like you too." Henry says. But I don't hear it.

Chapter 36

I give Mya a scowl & she smiles. "I am ready to call it a night." I say. Walking away with Phillip following behind me.

"Should I walk you to your room?" he asks.

"No thank you. I can see myself upstairs." I say handing him his suit jacket.

"Keep it. Next time you get cold, think of me." He says with a smile.

"This looks like a pretty expensive suit. Why would you want to split up the pieces?" I ask confused.

"It's fine Lana. I don't care. I hope to see you again soon." He says & kisses me on the cheek.

I see Henry walking towards the group & turn on my heels quickly. I hear Mya giggle in the background. Reminding myself to kill her later I keep walking.

I push my way through the now smaller crowd in the lounge & head upstairs.

The elevator ride feels like it takes forever but when I arrive on my floor I sprint to my door. My eyes feel as if they are welling up with tears. I am not sure why.

I open the door fling the jacket on my bed & strip out of Mya's clothes jumping into my bed. I roll onto my side & hug my pillow while tears stream down my cheek.

I started this trip feeling insecure & now I feel ten times worse. I reached for my phone to see if I have any missed texts from the kids & it was just one photo Carson & Clara sent me after dinner. They sent me a picture of their ice cream sundaes. I miss them. Being a mom is where my heart feels the fullest. Being home with my babies is where I long to be.

I dry my eyes on my pillowcase & sit up. My elbows on my knees & my face in my palms I let out a long sigh.

I stand up & throw on a pair shorts & my white t shirt & begin to pack my stuff. We only had one more day & night here. But I just want to go home. I want to leave & put this place & this week behind me.

My phone starts to ring & I turn around to see it say EXXXXX. Great. Now Derek is trying to drunk call me I assume. I ignore the call & continue folding my dresses & packing my things up.

Just as I finish folding my last piece of clothing from the closet the door swings open & laughter fills the room. I look over to the time on the clock in the room & it says 2:45 am.

"Really Mya feel free to make as much noise as you want at 3am." I say.

"Lana!" she shouts as she grabs my neck & kisses my forehead. "Why are you so serious all the time?" she asks.

"Mya, I am really not in the mood right now." I say.

"Are you ever?" she asks.

"Funny." I say.

"Serious." She says.

I take a deep breathe ready to deal with the current pain in my ass looking at me with glossy eyes & a huge smile on her face. When suddenly I hear the voices from the hallway.

"What the fuck are you doing?" I ask her.

"We are going to have a little after party. Want in?" she asks.

"No I want to climb back into the bed & go to sleep. One more day & then we head home." I say.

"One & half more days." She says rolling her eyes.

"Ok." I say. "same thing."

"God Lana, can you ever just relax. What is the problem you have a super-hot guy wanting to spend time with you & plus Henry is super jealous. I think you broke his little heart." She says in a condescending tone.

"You know what Mya. Grow the fuck up!" I shout & push her away from me.

She looks at me as if I just slapped her in the face.

"What the fuck is your problem?" she asks.

"You want to know what my problem is Mya Penelope? It's YOU & your nonsense. I am not this girl. I don't jump from guy to guy like you do." I say & instantly regret my cold words.

"Well, call me when you're done being a miserable bitch. Maybe you like being all alone Lana but some of us don't." she says & storms out slamming the door behind her.

I put my face in my hands & scream.

I lock the double lock on the door & climb into bed. I will be so happy when this week is over.

Chapter 37

I roll over & see the sun shining through the window. I have one eye open & check the clock next to me. It says 9:01 am.

I notice Mya is not in her bed & I roll over & put my face in my pillow.

She is pissed at me & rightfully so. I never should have said what I said to her last night. I was mad at myself & Henry. Not her.

I sit up & run my fingers through my hair. I reach for my phone & see a text from Clara & one from Derek.

"Hi mom. I passed the jr. counselor test!" – Clara

"L. Sorry about last night. Call me tonight." – D

I respond to Clara **with "I am so proud my beautiful girl. I knew you would. Miss & love you. How is Carson doing? Xo Mom."**

Then I ignore the text from Derek because I know this game he is playing. Derek has always been jealous even when I am not with him.

I stand & stretch. Walking to the closet I realize all of my clothes are packed up. I lift my suitcase to the bed & reach for my bright yellow & pink running shorts & matching top set. I slip into it & throw my messy hair into a ponytail. I slip into my "old lady sandals" as Mya calls them & head out the door after grabbing my phone & purse.

"Is the complimentary brunch buffet still going on?" I ask the nice woman at the desk.

"Yes miss. It will be available until 11 am." She says.

I walk into the lounge & see the extremely bright sunshine flowing in through the back doors. It looks gorgeous out on the beach & I can feel the heat already booming from outside.

I walk to the table & grab two fresh blueberry scones & load my plate up with fresh fruit as well. I grab a cup to fill with black coffee & walk out onto the patio. I see an empty table & chair in the corner of the patio facing the water.

Placing my cup & plate on the table I stretch once more & kick my shoes off under the table. I step down the steps onto the beach to feel the warm sand on my feet. I debate on walking to the edge of the water when I hear my name being called from behind me.

I turn to see Henry standing on the top step staring at me. "Morning." He says.

"Good morning." I say in a curt tone.

I walk past him & sit at my table thanking the heavens there is only one chair at my table. I take a bite of my scone & sip my black coffee avoiding eye contact with Henry.

"Sleep well?" he asks with his hands in his pockets.

"Fine." I say.

"Lana, look I know you think I was snooping but I wasn't I just wanted to plug your phone in for you so you didn't miss a call or text from your kids. I wasn't snooping. And I honestly don't care nor do I have a right to ask about your relationship with your ex. I like you.

And the only reason I was acting so off was because I was afraid of getting hurt by you." He says & looks away.

I stop chewing & put the blueberry scone down on my plate. "Afraid of being hurt by…..ME?" I ask questioningly.

"Yes." Henry says. "I like you a lot Lana. I know the last thing you need is some guy ruining your strong, independence." He says.

I sigh & cross my arms over my stomach. "I like you to Henry. I just…. I don't know what I want or what I'm even doing." I say.

"And that's okay. Because neither do I." he says.

I smile & hug myself tighter.

"I just know I want to see what happens with us. I don't want this to just be a one-night fling from the beach. I really want to know you & I want to see where this could go." He says.

I fucking hate myself in this moment. I thought he just wanted to Netflix & chill one night only or whatever Mya says about one-night stands. And here is this great guy asking to see where things go with me? What is happening this week. Could I be more appealing than I thought or is it just a fluke thing? Do people like gray haired, stress wrinkles & chubby thighs all of a sudden? Boy a lot has changed since I was in high school.

"Henry, I really like you too. But I'd be lying if I said I am looking for a commitment or anything serious when I have no idea what I am even doing in my own life. But just for the record no matter what happens I am not getting back with my ex. Ever." I say confidently.

Pretty much the one thing I do know for sure is that Derek is my past. Sure, at one point all I wanted was for my family to be whole again & my husband to come home & love me again. But I have

been reminded these past few days of my worth & who I once was
& still am. And for that I only have one person to thank.

Chapter 38

Mya;

I roll over & the sun is way to fucking bright. Sean is passed out in a chair by the window & Tommy is sound asleep sprawled on the bed next to me. Well, I got some sleep I guess & alone. Cheers to me for pulling that off.

I yawn & roll onto my back & pull my phone out from under me. It is officially 10 am. Great, I almost missed the free brunch. I need to eat like right now. I sit up & notice Sean is adjusting himself in the chair but he is still asleep. As is Tommy snoring away. I jump up & slip on my heels. Adjusting my dress I sneak by the chair. I write my number on a napkin on the table & say thanks for the fun. I want Sean to call me, but I am unsure of how I feel about Tommy. Normally Tommy is more my type but Sean kind of has that hot smart thing going for him. Plus, a southern accent always does it for me. But for some reason all I can think about is JC.

And what Lana said to me.

Chapter 39

I finish up my scones & coffee while Henry stands over me & sips his coffee.

I stand & wipe my face with my napkin. I reach up & hug Henry. His embrace is warm & inviting. I never noticed before but he smells like warm vanilla.

"So, call me?" I ask.

"You know I will." Henry smiles & kisses my forehead.

"Tonight is our last night & I need an early night to rest up from this mini vacay with Mya. Plus, I need some one-on-one time with her." I say.

"I understand. So Phillip Divine?" he says.

I crack up laughing. "I am still pretty star struck myself" I say blushing.

"Hey, I don't blame him. You are the most beautiful girl at the beach." He says to me.

I smile & hug him once more trying to inhale as much of his vanilla scent as I can.

I notice Mya strolling into the lounge in her heels, dress, & a big "KIRKLAND BEACH" sweatshirt. Which I assume she just purchased in the lobby.

Henry walks away & I power walk towards Mya. I reach her & she is loading her plate with bacon, eggs, sweets, & more. I grab her & pull her into me.

"I am so sorry for what I said last night Mya. I had no right to…." I say before Mya cuts me off.

"Do you think they have ice coffee included?" she asks.

"Mya, I am sorry." I say again.

"Yeah, I heard you. I don't accept it." She says continuing to load her plate & avoid eye contact with me.

"Mya. I am not going to have us fighting the last night of our vacation. So go ahead. Say whatever you want to me. I have it coming. Give me your best." I say.

She looks up from her plate & cocks her head to the side. "You wore that to make up with Henry? Honestly Lana, you think you would learn a thing or two from me this week." she says with a smirk on her face.

"I love you Mya." I say laughing.

She drops her plate on the table & turns & gives me a big hug. "I guess I love you too." She says holding me tight & laughing right along with me.

After Mya eats, we head upstairs & she takes her long awaited nap in her own bed after we shower & get cozy in our pjs. I call down & have room service delivered for us for dinner while Mya sleeps. I get all the pasta & pizza they have, along with 3 different types of dessert for each of us. I also order a bacon burger for Mya since she is a huge meat eater. Whereas I like the carbs a lot more.

The food is delivered & I poke Mya to let her know I got us some food.

"Mya I got you a bacon burger" I say.

She rolls onto her side & picks up the alarm clock. "Lana it's only 4:30. I wanted to sleep till 7. Why do you always have to eat at the early bird special with everyone's grandparents?" she asks, groaning, throwing her arm over her eyes.

"Sit up & let's eat. I also booked us a 7pm massage. They come right to our room!" I tell her.

"Okay, okay now you're talking." She says sitting up & throwing the covers off her.

"You know. I owe you an apology & a thank you." I say to Mya as I dive int the pasta bowl.

"Oh, why's that?" she asks sitting back down with her burger.

She grabs the remote to turn on some reality tv show about housewives that fight a lot.

"Well, you helped me a lot this week. If it wasn't for you, I wouldn't feel so confident & special." I say.

"Confident & special?" she says with a devilish grin.

"Yes, I was thinking earlier about how much you have done for me the past few days. You reminded me of who I am. I know I act like such a mom sometimes & I know you are not my child, but I love you & worry about you. Sometimes I just want to protect you from all the things I am afraid of." I say to her.

Mya looks up from her burger & the tv. "Lana, what could you possibly be afraid of? You are legit the strongest woman I have ever met. You're fearless. You carry yourself & your children on your own back & make magic out of messes. I look up to you. I just want you to have some fun because you deserve it." Mya says to me.

Tears well up in my eyes & I jump onto her bed & hug her tightly. "Boys like me still." I say & start to laugh in her neck as I hug her.

Mya pulls me tight & says "I know you big slut. You had quite a few admirers this weekend. Derek who?" she says back.

I smile at her & remember why she is my best friend. She is my soul mate.

Chapter 40

We spend the rest of the night enjoying relaxing massages & pig out on all the food. Mya has a few drinks but I decide not to since I am still feeling hungover from the night before.

I pack up the rest of our things while Mya sits on the balcony of our room under the stars. I watch her & think about our younger years. If it wasn't for Mya I wouldn't have made it through all the ups & downs with Derek & grams & nonna. Even with the kids. She's helped me in more ways than she will ever know.

I finish packing up & jump back on the bed with a cannoli & put on some rom com & drift off. Early morning for us tomorrow. We head home.

Chapter 41

Mya;

I sit on the balcony & watch the gorgeous stars in the sky. This place is fucking heaven. Note to self – buy beach property asap.

I look in as Lana flies around the room cleaning up after the two of us. She is such a badass. I wish she knew how amazing she really was. Sometimes it's like she takes care of everyone else so much she forgets herself. She always puts herself last on the list. It seems silly but she needs me to push her into doing it for herself. She deserves so much more than she knows. I only wish she saw it. But that's why she has me.

I sip my fruity drink & watch her in awe. She cares for me like a mother, a sister, a best friend. A soulmate. Lana has helped me in more ways than she will ever know. Always letting me be unapologetically, me.

Chapter 42

We load the car up & head back into to have brunch before we head out of Kirkland Beach. This place was a heaven sent. I have my suit on so I can dip in the water after brunch & maybe catch a few rays of sun. I told Mya it is best to leave around noon time when morning traffic is died down.

"Blueberry Scones are hot" Mya says as she hands me one.

"I think I will do an egg plate." I say with a smile.

"Ms. Lana are you going to change it up on the last day? You wild card full of adventure." Mya says with a boisterous laugh to follow.

We fill our plates, grab some coffee & make our way to the patio. Outside we are greeted by JC & Henry. They sit with us momentarily & we exchange our goodbyes & farewells. Mya gives JC a huge kiss & promises to keep in touch. JC says he will hold her to it.

Henry invites me & the kids to the Fields Farm whenever we would like to visit.

They are just about to walk away when JC turns back & steps up to Mya.

"I want to see you again." He says.

"Yeah, I just told you we would keep in touch." She says rolling her eyes at him.

"Not good enough." He says staring at her.

I look between the two of them. I am intrigued.

"What is your problem dude. Did you catch feelings that quick?" Mya says as she stands with a smirk.

JC grabs Mya & kisses her deeply. I even blush it is so intense.

"I want to see you again Mya. I like you. So tell me when & where." Says JC sternly.

"Okay, okay. Jeesh clingy much? Let's plan to meet for drinks next weekend." She says, catching her breathe from that wildly large show of affection.

"Okay." He says.

They walk away & Henry winks & blows a kiss my way before throwing his arm over JC's shoulder & rustling his hair. JC pulls away & looks back at Mya sticking his tongue out at her. Yupp they might be a perfect pair. I think to myself.

We were just about finished eating when Phillip came to our table.

"Lana." He says breathing shallow.

"Phillip, you're still here?" I ask.

"Never left. My sister & her new husband decided to rent the bungalow house on the beach for the next week. I figured I would stay as well." He says.

"Oh." I say.

"I remembered you said you were leaving today." He says.

"Yeah, we are all packed up. Just having breakfast & maybe a quick dip on the beach." I say smiling.

"May I join you?" he asks.

Before I can answer Mya clears our plates. "Go on get in the water. I am going to have seconds." She says with a wink.

I nudge her foot under the table. I know what she is playing at. I stand & help her with the plates.

"I will meet you at the water." I tell Phillip.

"Sure thing." He says.

"Mya what the fuck are you doing? You know I like Henry." I say.

"Lana, live a little. Swimming with a cute guy isn't sleeping with him. And who said you were dating Henry? Don't you deserve to have a little fun & have options?" she asks.

"I guess so." I say.

I walk off & head towards Phillip slipping out of my dress to dive in the water with him.

We spent a beautiful morning on the beach before heading home.

I say goodbye to Phillip who also asks me to see him again & stay in touch. In fact, he invites me to New York.

I am in shock at all that has happened this week. And the person I have to thank is Mya.

We get in the car & head home Mya asked me to drive so she can sip her end of vacation drinks. I love this wild girl.

As I drive home & watch the trees pass, I can't help but think of Derek. I am not sure why, but my mind is stuck on Derek & the kids.

We drive for over an hour & finally make it home. Mya jumps out of the car & tells me she's staying over my house tonight, so she doesn't need to drive anymore. Even though I drove us home.

She climbs into my bed with me & we try to decompress from the past week. I text the kids & tell them I love them. I text Derek & let him know I am home (again not sure why but he is on my mind.) I look at my phone & notice both Henry & Phillip have text me.

Drive Safely & The offer stands for the farm, anytime Lana. I hope to see you very soon. That was the best night of my life. – Henry

Let me know when you arrive home safely. I hope you will visit me in New York. I can't stop thinking about you & that kiss. – Phillip

Good God. How did I go from hating my looks, my body, my life to being involved with two new men, & my ex is clearly trying to re connect with me. I look over at Mya as she sleeps in my bed taking up most of it. "I blame you." I whisper.

Chapter 43

I roll over & Mya isn't next to me in the bed. Instead, I instantly smell bacon being cooked in my house. Which is funny because I don't buy or eat bacon. I hear her music blasting from the kitchen downstairs.

"Mya good god it is 5am. Even I am not up yet." I whisper shout to her.

She spins around in my bathrobe & I notice she is using my super expensive organic mud mask.

"Shit sorry Lana. I have been up all-night thinking of how fun this trip was." She says.

"Yeah it was great." I say.

"You pick a guy yet?" she asks.

"I think I know who I am going to go see." I say.

I sit at my countertop & brush off the crumbs from Mya's toast she made.

"Where did you get the bacon?" I ask.

"oh, I ran to the all night convenience. Who the fuck doesn't have bacon Lana?" Mya asks.

"I have bacon Mya." I say as I roll my eyes.

"Turkey bacon isn't bacon." Mya scoffs.

"Ok but that stuff smells disgusting." I say.

She laughs. "So I was thinking. Since we had so much fun on this trip & I was able to get you out…" she says pausing to look at me.

"Yeah?" I ask worriedly.

"I booked us another trip to a tropical island for November!!!!!" she shouts.

"WHAT!?!?!" I shout, jumping out of my seat.

"YUPP, GET READY FOR OUR HOLIDAY TRIP TO THE TROPICAL COAST." She says with a grin. "Already booked & paid for. I figured why not we just had the best time right?" she asks.

"Mya, November is a busy time for me. That's almost Christmas." I say.

"Pick a guy Lana. Because I got us 4 tickets to paradise." She says.

"A guy?" I ask. "Wait this isn't just us?" I say.

"Nope." She says with a wink.

"And what guy are you bringing?" I ask.

"Depends on you." She says.

"What? Why?" I ask.

"I can't invite the opposite friend of who you invite." She says.

I sit back down & drop my head on the table. I look at my phone & realize I have   3 more texts.

Derek.

Henry.

Phillip.

Well now what the fuck do I do?

Mya slides a plate of eggs & toast over to me with no bacon. She pours my orange juice & slides it over to me.

"Think fast Lana. We are going to the islands & we are bringing dates. HO, HO, HO." She says with a smile.

I am royally screwed.

I guess we are doing it all over again. I think to myself sipping my juice.

You never know what you're going to get with Mya. That's why I love her.

Author's Note

If you enjoyed Forever Friends; The good, the bad, the beach then be on the look out for the next book in the series. "Forever Friends; Jingle, Jangle, Jungle" will be available sometime this year.

Thank you for coming on this wild adventure with Lana & Mya. I hope you love them as much as I do. And just wait because they have many more adventures to come.

Thank you to everyone who took the time out to read this book. I appreciate you so much. I am always open to feedback. So kindly share your reviews with me on social media!

You can find me on Instagram under
@_Livinglifewithlydia_

www.ingramcontent.com/pod-product-compliance
Lightning Source LLC
Chambersburg PA
CBHW070457170726

48291CB00008B/2552